FOLK TALES AND HEROES
OF WALES

Volume 3

Folk Tales and Heroes of Wales

Volume 3

John Owen Huws
Illustrations: Catrin Meirion
Adapted by Siân Lewis

© Text: Helen Huws
First published in Welsh in 2001

Copyright © by Gwasg Carreg Gwalch 2006

ISBN: 1-84527-024-X

Cover illustrations: Catrin Meirion
Cover design: Sian Parri

Published with the financial support
of the Welsh Books Council.

Published by
Gwasg Carreg Gwalch, 12 Iard yr Orsaf, Llanrwst,
Wales LL26 0EH.
✆ 01492 642031   📄 01492 641502
✆ books@carreg-gwalch.co.uk   Web site: www.carreg-gwalch.co.uk

Contents

ThE MAGIC
OINTMENT

The square at Caernarfon is famous throughout Wales. There you will hear the people of Caernarfon – the 'Cofis' – chatting to each other in their own rich dialect. At one end of the square stands an enormous castle built by Edward 1 after Prince Llywelyn the Last had been killed by his men over seven hundred years ago. At the other end stands an enormous Post Office which is nowhere near as old!

In fact the Post Office isn't old at all. Not so long ago a mound stood there. The mound was flattened when the Slate Quay was built in the shade of the castle wall. So the town gained a huge quay and a huge square at one and the same time – just by demolishing a mound of earth!

If you look at old photographs of Caernarfon, you will see the mound where the Post Office now stands. The mound was the site of Caernarfon fair for hundreds of years and Caernarfon fair is where this story begins.

*   *   *

It was the month of October many years ago. Abel Prydderch and his wife Mali, who lived on a small farm called Garth Dorwen outside Pen-y-groes in the Nantlle Valley, were feeling rather sorry for themselves.

'I'm not one to grumble, Abel, as you well know,' said Mali. 'But I do feel the work on the farm is getting too much for me.'

'Maybe so,' Abel replied carefully. 'We're not getting any younger, you and I.'

'It's not my age, Abel. There just aren't enough hours in a day. Even though I get up at the crack of dawn, I still can't cope with all the ironing, the washing, the churning and the baking.'

'That's true,' said Abel, 'I'd noticed that things were getting on top of you.' Mali had been feeding him bread and cheese twice daily for weeks on end, so no wonder he'd noticed. Still he didn't complain, because he thought the world of his wife and didn't want to offend her.

'How about getting a maid to help me?' suggested Mali.

'That's a good idea. The maid can churn, wash, sweep and scrub and you can spend your time cooking.'

'You're not grumbling, are you?'

'No, no,' said Abel hastily. 'But I wouldn't mind a

plate of stew or an apple tart every now and then.'

'Is that so? Well, I dare say you'll have plenty of both before long,' said Mali.

'Why is that?'

'It's almost time for the November Fair in Caernarfon. Don't tell me you've forgotten. All the serving-maids and farm hands will be looking for new employment.'

'Oh yes, of course,' said Abel. 'With luck we'll find a good little maid at the fair. Good idea, old girl.'

'Old? You watch it, my lad!' retorted Mali. 'Don't forget you're three years older than I am!' And the two of them chuckled happily. They were so pleased to have found an answer to their problem.

When fair day came, Abel and Mali put on their best clothes, harnessed their mare, Bess, to the cart and set off for Caernarfon to find a hardworking maid.

'Goodness me, I've never seen so many people,' said Abel as he tried to steer Bess through the crowds on the square.

'Yes, everybody and his sister is here today,' said Mali. 'We're sure to find a maid.'

'And I'm sure to find a bargain in the cattle sale,' replied Abel. 'Why don't you go and have a look round the cloth and china stalls near the castle, while I go and ask the price of a horned cow?'

'You'll do no such thing!' said Mali firmly. 'We came here to look for a maid and that's what we're going to do. I know your tricks. You'll have bought a cow and a calf before I turn round and then we won't have enough money to hire a maid.'

'All right, Mali,' sighed Abel. He was so excited at the thought of the cattle sale he'd completely forgotten all those miserable meals of bread and cheese.

'The servants are all standing on that mound over there waiting to be hired. We'll go over there now before your money burns a hole in your pocket,' said Mali.

Although they could see the mound, it wasn't easy to get to it on that particular day. Hundreds and hundreds of people had flocked to the fair to spend their few pence. There were plenty of things to tempt them and plenty of people willing to take their money.

'Look! There's Blind Dafydd, the balladeer,' said Abel. 'Listen to him! He's selling a ballad on that murder in Dolgellau for a penny.'

'Oh Abel, you could spend a fortune here in two shakes, what with all the silks, the medicines, the china . . .'

'I know! And listen to that man over there. He's offering the wonders of the world for three pence. He's got a dog with two heads, a bearded lady and the tallest man in the world. Let's go and have a look.'

'No, Abel! First we find a maid, then we can wander round the fair in our own time. I'll be going to that gipsy caravan to hear my fortune and you can go and see the boxing match behind the Black Boy Inn. But before we do that, we've got to find a maid!'

'You're quite right, Mali.'

By this time they had reached the mound where the servants were standing. The men stood on one side and the women on the other. Farmers in their best clothes wandered in between the two rows and now and then bargains were struck with a slapping of hands.

'Have you made your choice yet, Mali?' asked Abel.

'No. Have you?'

'Not really. If I needed a farm hand, it would be easy.

10

There are plenty of sturdy young lads.'

'Yes, there are. But the maids are more suited to the posh houses in town. They don't look like farm maids at all.'

'No . . . wait a minute, Mali. How about that one over there?'

'Which one? The one who's standing on her own? Yes, she looks strong and healthy.'

'She won't be afraid of hard work,' said Abel.

'There's only one way to find out,' replied Mali. 'I'll go and ask her.'

And so she did. They soon learnt that the name of the girl was Eilian and that she came from Nant y Betws. She was looking for farm work, because she liked living in the country. The three of them took a liking to each other and struck a bargain there and then. Abel gave Eilian a shilling for luck and arranged for her to start work at Garth Dorwen at eight o'clock the following Monday morning, then the three of them wandered off to enjoy the fair.

That afternoon, both Eilian and Mali went to have their fortune told. The gipsy told Eilian that she would go on a journey to a distant land and Mali was told she would be drawn into an adventure that would endanger her life. They both laughed. They thought the gipsy was making it up as she gazed into her crystal ball. Little did they realise that her words would come true.

*　　*　　*

The following Monday Eilian arrived at Garth Dorwen and, just as Abel and Mali had predicted, she was an excellent worker. She never tired and would sing away from morning till night. She was an expert at churning and she made the best butter in the Nantlle Valley. Now Mali had time to prepare Abel's favourite meals and soon she was teasing him that he was as fat as mud. He laughed happily and replied:

'I'll tell you one thing. We were very lucky to get hold of Eilian before someone else snapped her up.'

'We were indeed. She's a maid in a million.'

'Yes. And I've never seen anyone take such pleasure in her work,' said Abel.

'There's only one thing I can't understand,' said Mali with a frown. 'Why on earth does she go out to spin every night?'

'What's wrong with that?'

'Well, think about it, Abel. It's the middle of winter. No one in her right mind goes outside to spin at this time of year.'

'You'd swallow anything, Mali!' laughed Abel. 'She's not spinning! She's met a young man in Pen-y-groes, I bet you anything.'

'Do you think so? She always brings back a heap of wool.'

'I'm sure she does. I know she works hard, but the best worker in the world couldn't spin wool on the fields of Garth Dorwen in January, when the nights are pitch dark! And besides it's freezing cold and all sensible people are huddled in front of the fire. I'm sure that's what Eilian is doing too. I bet you she's huddled in front of a fire at this very moment, only it's not ours!'

'Well, if that's true, I hope she's not thinking of leaving us. She's such a good worker, I don't want to lose her now,' said Mali.

But they did lose Eilian. She went out more and more often and stayed out longer and longer. And then, one night, she did not come back.

Abel and Mali didn't sleep a wink that night. They called their dog, took a lantern and searched every inch of the fields, but there was no sign of Eilian.

Next morning Mali went to Pen-y-groes to ask if anyone knew what had happened to her. She came back in great dismay. No one had seen her and she had not been meeting any of the local young men. That afternoon Abel rode round the mountain to Nant y Betws to see if the maid had run home. Her family were astonished to see him. They hadn't seen Eilian since she started work at Garth Dorwen, but she had written many times to say how happy she was on the farm and how fond she was of Abel and Mali. There was no trace of Eilian anywhere. It was as if the earth had opened and swallowed her up.

*　　*　　*

As the months went by the people of the locality forgot Eilian, but Abel and Mali never stopped thinking about her. Mali had to do all housework and once again Abel was living on bread and cheese.

Mali was a midwife, as well as being a farmer's wife. A midwife is a woman who helps mothers at the birth of their children. One moonlit night there was a knock on the door.

'Who on earth can be bothering us at this time of night?' grumbled Abel.

'What time is it?' asked Mali.

'Five to eleven.'

There was another knock. When Mali went to open the door, Abel heard a man's voice.

'Good evening. Are you Mali Prydderch?'

'Yes, sir,' she replied.

'Our visitor must be a very important man, if Mali's calling him "sir",' murmured Abel. He went to peep round the door.

'My wife is expecting a baby at any moment,' said the visitor. 'Can you come and help?'

'Certainly. Let me put on my cloak.'

While Mali hurried to fetch her cloak, Abel took a good look at the stranger. He was dressed in black from head to foot. The cloth was rich and very different from any cloth that Abel had ever seen. His horse was so dark as to be almost invisible, even though the full moon was shining on the farmyard.

Abel tried to strike up a conversation.

'Have you travelled far, sir?' he asked.

'Not really,' was the stranger's terse reply.

Abel was surprised, because he knew all the local people and he had never seen this man before. By this time Mali had returned and the stranger addressed her.

'If you get up behind me on my horse, we'll go at once to my wife. You don't mind, do you?'

'I don't mind at all,' said Mali. And off they went.

Abel closed the door and went to bed, but he could not sleep. There was something strange about the visitor on the black horse, but he couldn't think what it was.

Abel would have been astonished if he'd known the truth. Mali herself couldn't believe her eyes. Instead of taking her to a faraway mansion, the stranger headed for nearby Rhos y Cowrt and rode towards a hill called Bryn

y Pibion. Though Mali knew the place well, she had never noticed the dark cave in the hillside till the horse galloped inside.

She was even more amazed to see lights glowing at the far end of the cave. They were the lights of a magnificent palace! The stranger led her through the palace doorway into a room that sparkled with gold and silver. At one end a fire blazed in a marble grate and opposite the fire was a bed of pure gold with a mattress of the softest feathers spread with silken sheets. A young woman lay there.

'This is my wife,' the stranger said. 'Will you help her?'

'I'll take great care of her,' said Mali.

'Thank you. I shall return once the baby is born, and if you do your work well, you shall be richly rewarded.'

'Thank you, sir.'

Well, the baby was safely delivered and as soon as he let out a cry, the stranger returned. In his hand he carried a small bottle of ointment.

'Mali Prydderch,' he said. 'I want you to dab the ointment on the baby's eyes. You must take care not to let it touch your own eyes. Do you understand?'

'Yes, sir.'

'Very well. After you have done so, call me. You'll have your money and I shall take you back to Garth Dorwen.'

Mali dipped her little finger in the ointment and smeared it onto the baby's eyes. As she did so, she felt a tickle in the corner of her right eye. Without thinking, she rubbed it with the very same finger that she'd dipped in the ointment!

At once, the vision in her right eye changed. Instead of

a fine palace she saw a dark, damp cave with a smoky fire. Instead of a golden bed, she saw a heap of straw. But the greatest surprise was still to come. She looked at the young mother who was lying on the straw and cried out.

'Eilian! It's you!'

'Sh, my dear mistress! Please don't raise your voice or we shall be in grave trouble. How did you recognise me?'

'Some of the ointment got into my eye, but don't worry about that. Are you all right, Eilian, my dear?'

'Yes, I am – but you won't be, once my husband knows you've recognised me. In fact I doubt he'll let you go.'

'But who is he?'

'He's one of the Fairy Folk.'

'The Fairy Folk!' gasped Mali.

'Sh, mistress! Listen to me. Pretend you don't know me and you'll leave here a rich woman. If you don't, you'll be here for ever.'

'Eilian, come with me, I beg of you.'

'I can't. Don't say a word. Just call my husband or he'll suspect something's up.'

With a heavy heart Mali did as she was told and the stranger took her back to Garth Dorwen. As he left, he gave her a purse stuffed with gold.

* * *

Once again the months flew by. In the meantime life had changed for Abel and Mali. With the fairy gold they were able to employ another maid and buy any food that tickled Abel's fancy, so he could eat to his heart's content.

One day, Mali went to the market that was held on the square in Caernarfon and as she went from stall to stall, she noticed that the man in front of her was taking things from the stalls and sliding them into the pockets of his black suit.

No one else could see the thief and Mali suddenly realised why. She herself could only see him through one eye – the eye in which she'd rubbed the ointment. She decided to go up and challenge him, but as she did so she saw his face. To her shock and surprise he was Eilian's husband. The thief was the rich man who had given her so much gold.

In her confusion she called out: 'How is Eilian?'

'She's very well, thank you,' said the man with a sly glance. 'With which eye can you see me?'

'This one,' said Mali, pointing to her right eye.

At once the man in black picked up a reed from the floor and with it he blinded Mali's right eye.

That was the last time that Mali saw the Fairy Folk, but she often remembered the words of the gipsy long ago. For both Eilian and herself those words had come true.

*　　*　　*

Although the hill where Mali first met Eilian has long since disappeared, the market is still held on the square every Saturday. Maybe the Fairy Folk still wander from stall to stall, but no one can see them any more.

The field where Eilian first met the Fairies can still be seen at Garth Dorwen. It is called Cae Eilian, or Eilian's

Field. But there's no sign of the cave where she lived, though the hill is still there.

If you saw a cave, would you be brave enough to creep inside? I wouldn't . . .

GUTO NYTH BRÂN

If you visit Mountain Ash you will see a memorial to one of Wales's most famous heroes, the runner Guto Nyth Brân. His real name was Griffith Morgan and he lived in Nyth Brân in the parish of Llanwynno in the Rhondda Valley. He is remembered as the greatest runner Wales has ever seen. He may well have been one of the fastest runners of all time. He was born in the year 1700 and died when he was thirty-seven years old in 1737. Though his life was short, people still talk about his extraordinary feats. I'm sure you'd like to hear about them too.

* * *

Three hundred years ago Nyth Brân was a simple cottage. Like many other cottages around Pontypridd it was built of rough stone and the walls were whitewashed. The land around it was coarse mountain pasture, which was only good for keeping sheep – and that was exactly what Guto's father did with his son's help.

Even when he was a tiny boy, Guto loved running. The other children could never catch him when they played tag and, according to his mother, he flew so fast over the grass that the blades barely bent beneath his feet. Nothing ever slowed him down – neither gate nor hedge, wood nor bog – and he could run like a hare over the mountainsides. He always ran over the mountains in a straight line no matter how steep they were.

'Will you go over to Aberdare to buy me some yeast, Guto?' his mother asked one morning. 'I've got to do some baking and I've none left. So will you go later on, please?'

'I'll go now, Mam,' Guto replied.

'No, don't go now. You haven't had your breakfast yet, boy.'

'Don't worry, Mam. You fill the kettle and start preparing breakfast. I'll be back by the time it's ready.'

'But it's twelve miles to Aberdare and back!'

'I know, but it won't take me long if I go over the mountain. See you soon! 'Bye!'

Off went Guto over hill and dale, as fast as if he were running on flat ground. It took a while for his mother to prepare breakfast for a house full of starving children. As she was finishing cooking and laying the table, Guto tore into the yard waving the packet of yeast.

Guto loved running over the mountains and never lost his footing however steep and rocky they were. One day his mother sent him on another message to Aberdare, while she popped next door to Hafod to see her friend. When she returned home, Guto was sitting on the settle by the fire.

'Now Guto,' she said impatiently, 'I asked you to go to Aberdare and here you are lazing around in front of the fire. Off you go now instead of wasting time.'

'Wasting time! I've been to Aberdare and back while you were gossiping,' protested Guto. 'Look in the pantry if you don't believe me.'

'Oh, goodness me!' his mother said. 'I'm very sorry Guto. I didn't realise I'd spent so much time chatting.'

'It wasn't that long, Mam. It only took me an hour.'

Then at shearing time his father asked him to round up the sheep.

'Will you go up to the top of Gwyngul Mountain?' he asked. 'Some of the Hafod boys are coming over to help us with the shearing, so we need to bring the sheep down as soon as possible.'

'I'm on my way,' said Guto, jumping up.

'Take the dogs with you. It'll save you time,' said his father.

'I don't think so!' laughed Guto. 'I'll be faster without them.'

'Don't be so silly, boy. A shepherd needs a dog. And we're pressed for time today, so you'd better take both our dogs.'

'I promise you the sheep will down by mid-morning,' Guto replied.

He kept his promise. By mid-morning the yard was

full of bleating sheep. Guto's family rushed out just in time to see him close the gate behind them.

'You must have had a hard time without a dog to help you,' said his father.

'It wasn't too bad,' replied Guto. 'The only sheep I had trouble with was that little grey one in the corner.'

'A grey sheep! I've never seen a grey sheep. Where is it?'

'It's hiding behind that lamb over there.'

'But that's a hare, lad!' his father cried.

'Is it really?' said Guto innocently. Behind his father's back he aimed a sly wink at his mother and the Hafod boys.

'How did you catch the hare, Guto?' they all wanted to know.

'I saw her in the ferns on Llwyncelyn mountain,' he replied. 'I managed to catch her before she ran onto Hafod's land. From then on she had no choice but to run with the flock.'

'I've never seen anything like it!' said his father in amazement. 'Would anyone like to buy two good sheepdogs? We don't need them any more. We've got Guto.'

*   *   *

Soon Guto began to take part in races – and win. This is how it all began. He liked to go fox-hunting, but he would never dream of going on horseback. No, Guto preferred to run on his own two feet. He said he was faster and safer on foot, because the horses had to ride over rough terrain. Guto himself was quite used to running across country. In fact they say he was faster than the hounds and caught several foxes himself by grabbing their tails.

One day Guto had gone hunting with the Llanwynno hounds. They picked up the scent of a fox and chased it all the way from Glamorgan to Ceredigion. It was an astonishing run and at the end of it Guto, two hounds and the fox were the only ones left standing. The other hounds and the horses had given up in exhaustion.

Guto himself was so tired that neither he nor the two hounds had the strength to catch the fox. The lucky fox escaped with its life and Guto spent the night in the house of a gentleman who had witnessed the strange sight.

That night, after a bath and a fine meal, Guto told the gentleman his story. The stranger had his own story to tell.

'I'm afraid I won't have this house for much longer, Guto,' he said sadly. 'My family has owned it for hundreds of years, but I can no longer afford to keep it.'

'Why is that?' asked Guto.

'I placed a huge bet on a race between my horse and another gentleman's horse,' sighed his friend. 'Unfortunately the gentleman was no gentleman at all. He managed to slip a sleeping draught into my horse's food, so the animal could barely keep its eyes open throughout the race. I lost all my money and now I shall have to sell all I have to pay my debts.'

'Wait a minute,' said Guto. 'Don't be in too much of a hurry. I've an idea.'

'What is it? I'd do anything to save this mansion.'

'Let me challenge the man's horse to a race. You can

then bet twice as much money on me.'

'But, Guto, I have no money. And what if you lose?'

'I won't lose,' promised Guto, 'so you won't have to pay anything. In fact you'll have twice your money back from the cheat.'

The race was run and, just as Guto had said, he won handsomely and made a huge amount of money for the kind man who'd given him such a welcome in Ceredigion.

From then on Guto became famous and he was invited – or challenged – to race all over the country. He practised hard by running up and down the hills of the Rhondda Valley. He also had another, much stranger, training technique. The night before a big race he would sleep on a dung heap! According to Guto the dung heap was wonderfully warm and kept his body strong and supple. I wouldn't advise you to try it, though!

Many people made a fortune by betting on Guto. One of these was his girlfriend Siân, who kept a shop near Nyth Brân. She had great faith in his abilities and they thought the world of each other.

Soon people were offering Guto huge sums to take part in races. Once he was offered five hundred pounds – which would be thousands and thousands in today's money – if he could beat an army officer in a four mile race. The organisers knew that no one could beat Guto in a long distance race, but they thought the English soldier would beat him over a short distance. They were wrong. The race took place near Hirwaun and Guto won easily.

*   *   *

One day, when Guto was in Siân's shop, a messenger

brought him an important letter. It had to be important, because few people received letters in those days.

'I wonder who's written to me?' said Guto.

'Open it and see,' said Siân. 'It must be from a rich person, because the paper looks expensive and it's been brought by a personal messenger.'

Little did Guto know, as he broke the seal, that this would be the most important letter of his whole life. He was obviously delighted with its contents, because his face broke into a smile.

'Good news?' asked Siân.

'Very good,' he replied. 'Listen to this:

"Dear Guto,

I hear you're quite a fast runner, but I believe I have the fastest horse in all of Britain. To prove this I challenge you to run twelve miles against me at a place of your choosing. If you can beat me – which I doubt – I am prepared to pay you £1,000.

If you accept my challenge, I shall be visiting Caerphilly next week and we'll arrange the details then.

Yours faithfully,
John Prince"'

'You'll accept, I suppose?' said Siân.

'Yes, of course, I will. If I win this race, I'll have enough money to buy my own little farm – and maybe find a little woman who's willing to join me,' replied Guto with a wink.

'We'll see about that,' she laughed. 'First you have to win.'

The following week Guto went to Caerphilly accompanied by many of his friends. He accepted Prince's challenge and agreed that the race would take place in a month's time over a twelve mile course starting at Newport and finishing at Bedwas church near Caerphilly.

That race was the talk of South Wales for the whole of that month. Crowds came to watch Guto practise. This would be the race of the century – a race between the champion of Wales and the fastest horse in England. Needless to say the people of Rhondda were backing Guto and betting large amounts of money that he would win. His girlfriend, Siân, bet an apronful of gold sovereigns. During that month the runner was invited to sleep on many a dung heap. Everyone wanted to make sure he would win the race and win the locals a fortune!

At last the great day came. Crowds thronged round the starting line in Newport to watch Guto arrive, followed by Prince on his fine white horse.

'Are you ready?' called the mayor.

The two runners nodded.

BANG! At the sound of the mayor's pistol Guto and the horse raced off towards Caerphilly.

To the astonishment of the huge crowd Prince was in the lead before they'd left Newport. Guto didn't seem to be trying too hard and was soon left behind.

The race continued in this way for mile after mile with Guto jogging along and Prince stretching his lead. By the time Guto reached the half way mark, his supporters were very worried.

'What's wrong, Guto? Have you got a stitch in your side?' they called to him.

'Would you like a drink of water?'

'Would you like something stronger?'

'Are you all right?'

And what did Guto do? He stopped to chat to them. They couldn't believe it!

'There's no hurry, friends,' Guto said cheerfully. 'I'll catch up with Prince in no time and pass him too. Now where's that drink of water?'

'Here it is,' called a voice from the crowd. 'But please be quick about it. I've bet all this week's wages on you.'

'Well, in that case I'd better get a move on,' said Guto jokingly. 'I don't want you and Siân to lose your money. And I wouldn't mind winning a thousand pounds myself.'

After teasing his supporters, Guto began to run in earnest. He made up ground fast, but there was still a mile to go. Bedwas church was already in sight. Could he make it?

Yes, said his supporters. No way, said Prince's supporters – and to make sure they smashed bottles and scattered glass across Guto's path, hoping that the shards would slice through his thin running shoes. But Guto picked up speed and leapt over the obstacle with ease. When Prince's supporters saw him make such huge leaps, they were beside themselves, because they knew there was nothing they could do to stop him now.

Soon Guto was close on Prince's heels and when they got to the steep hill that leads up to Bedwas Church, they were neck and neck. The horse was galloping hard. It was doing its best to get away from Guto, but it was a losing battle.

Guto began to talk to Prince.

'How are you now then, Mr Prince? Isn't it a fine day?'

'Y . . . yes!' the man panted as he tried to spur his horse up the hill.

'Are you enjoying yourself?' Guto teased.

'Y..y..yes,' croaked Prince, who barely had the strength to speak.

'Excellent. I'm glad to hear it. I'd like nothing better than to chat to you, but I've got a race to win. Cheerio!'

And off went Guto as fast as a greyhound. He burst through the tape across the graveyard gate exactly fifty-three minutes after leaving Newport. He had run the twelve miles in well under an hour and in so doing he had beaten the fastest horse in England.

The crowd went wild. Their hero had won once again!

'Hooray! Hooray!'

'Well done, Guto lad!'

'Bless you, Guto. You've made my fortune today!'

Then Guto saw Siân coming towards him with open arms.

'Congratulations, Guto!' she said, wrapping her arms around him and giving him a hearty slap on the back.

Guto dropped dead on the spot. He had run hard over the last few miles and Siân's friendly pat was more than he could take. His heart stopped beating.

*   *   *

Siân won two apronfuls of gold sovereigns that day, but they meant nothing to her. She would have given anything to have Guto back.

She used some of the money to buy a gravestone for Guto. Carved on it were his name, his age and also the picture of a heart – to show how he died and to prove that she loved him.

If Guto were alive today, he would no doubt win many Olympic medals. As it is, his name and memory have never died. Not only is there a memorial to him in Mountain Ash, but there is also a race in his honour on New Year's Eve – a race dedicated to the memory of the fastest runner Wales has ever seen.

THE LOST BRIDE

In a steep valley high above the sea in Gwynedd stands the village of Nant Gwrtheyrn. It is the home of the National Language Centre where people from all over Wales – and the world – come to learn Welsh. If it had not been for the language centre, Nant Gwrtheyrn would have fallen into ruin. Until recently a rough path was the only means of reaching the village. It was a place where time had stood still.

Yet Nant Gwrtheyrn has a history that spans many centuries. In the story of King Vortigern and the fighting dragons, the King himself took refuge in this valley in the shadow of the Eifl mountain. And this is where he died, when his palace was struck by lightning and burnt to the ground. Nant Gwrtheyrn suffered many violent thunderstorms in days long ago.

Later on, before the days of the quarrymen who made their home in Nant Gwrtheyrn, men came to farm the valley. Our story belongs to that distant time. It tells of two young people called Rhys and Meinir. Would you like to hear it?

*   *   *

Years ago Nant Gwrtheyrn was a fine place in which to live. Although the path that led to it was steep and rocky, and although the rock of Craig Ddu was dark and threatening, the little valley itself was pleasant and welcoming. It was protected on three sides by mountains and sheltered from all winds except the winds from the sea. A traveller heading down towards the village would see spread out below him a patchwork of neat well-tended fields clustered around whitewashed farmhouses. The sheep looked like scraps of cotton wool on the slopes. Beyond them was the sea. All heavy goods were brought to Nant Gwrtheyrn by sea and you can imagine the excitement whenever a ship sailed in from Liverpool or Dublin and began to unload its cargo on the beach. The village school would be closed for the day as everyone rushed to lend a hand.

On neighbouring farms in Nant Gwrtheyrn lived two young people called Rhys and Meinir. For as long as they could remember the two had been in love. This was hardly surprising. Meinir was very pretty. She had bright golden hair that shone in the sun and she was never without a smile on her face. She was everyone's favourite. Rhys had a mop of black, curly hair and he too was as happy as a lark. He was always full of mischief and people liked him for it.

There was another very special reason why Rhys and Meinir were so fond of each other. One fine afternoon a crowd of children had gone to play on the banks of the little stream that flows through the valley. While the girls went to play houses, Siôn Ty Pella said to the boys, 'Let's dam up the stream and catch the fish that are left in the pool.'

'Yes! Good idea!' said Rhys. 'We can swim in the pool too!'

That afternoon, beneath a hot sun, the children shifted heaps of earth and stones. The girls used the stones to build a house, while the boys built a dam. They worked so hard, they barely said a word for an hour or more, which was very unusual. The only noise was the hum of the bees, the popping of the gorse in the heat and an occasional groan when a boy picked up a stone that was far too heavy for him. The stream fell silent as the dam grew and the boys sealed it with earth and pebbles.

'The dam's big enough now,' said Rhys at last.

'Right!' said Siôn. 'Off we go to check on the fish.'

And off they went along the riverbank in one big happy gang. There were six of them in all and they listened carefully for the sounds of a trout struggling in an inch of water. The girls took no notice. They had better things to do, such as gathering shells to make a tea set.

An hour later the boys came back, each one with a fish in his arms.

'Look, Meinir,' said Rhys. 'This trout weighs at least a pound. My dad will enjoy this tonight.'

'Ugh, Rhys!' she cried. 'Take it away!'

'But I thought you liked fish.'

'I do, but only after Mam has cleaned and fried them.'

'Huh! Girls!' said Rhys to the other boys.

The boys left their fish in a puddle so they wouldn't dry out, then off they went to swim in the deep pool beside the dam. The girls kept away. They were enjoying themselves.

Later that afternoon, when it was almost time to go home, Meinir heard her mother calling to her.

'Meinir! Tea's ready! Meinir!'

'Coming, Mam!' she replied.

The fastest way home was over the dam. Crossing the dam would save her walking a quarter of a mile upstream to the wooden bridge, so she rushed towards it without thinking.

'Watch out!' shouted Rhys. 'The dam isn't...'

Before the words were out of his mouth, the stones crumpled beneath Meinir's weight and with a scream, the girl fell into the pool.

Everyone looked on in dismay. Then Gwyneth Ty'n Llwyn found her voice.

'She can't swim!' she yelled. 'Meinir can't swim!'

At once Rhys plunged into the depths of the pool. He caught hold of Meinir and pulled her out. Despite being pale and shocked, she managed a shy smile.

'Thank you, Rhys,' she said.

'Oh, it was nothing,' said Rhys, but he blushed all the same.

From that day on Rhys and Meinir knew they were meant for each other. Meinir was an only child. Her mother died when she was young and she was the apple of her father's eye. Ever since the day Rhys rescued Meinir, her father thought the world of Rhys too and treated him like a son. Rhys's family thought no less of Meinir.

*   *   *

Their feelings never changed. Throughout their school days Rhys and Meinir remained true to each other. They carved hearts on trees and scratched their initials inside. They were so much in love that no one was surprised when one day they announced their engagement. The two families were delighted.

'Who is the oldest person in the valley?' Meinir's father asked.

'William Cae'r Nant,' said Rhys. 'Why do you ask?'

'You know what happens when two people get engaged, don't you, Rhys? You've heard of the broomstick ceremony?'

'Oh yes, of course.'

The next day William Cae'r Nant, who was one hundred years old, came to Meinir's house followed by most of the people of the valley. Rhys and Meinir waited for him with smiles on their faces. William had a broom in his hand fashioned from the twigs of the oldest oak in the valley. According to tradition the young people had to jump over it. It was a sign that they intended to marry very soon.

'When will the wedding be, Meinir?' asked Siôn.

'Three months next Saturday, on Midsummer Day. Isn't that right, Rhys?'

'Yes,' said Rhys. 'And I'd like you to be my best man, Siôn. Will you?'

'Of course I will. Thanks for asking me?'

'And I'd like you, Gwyneth, to be my bridesmaid,' said Meinir. 'Will you?'

'I'd love to.'

Everyone went home happily. In three months' time they'd have a wedding to celebrate and weddings were great fun in Nant Gwrtheyrn.

*   *   *

Three weeks before the wedding a strange man was seen walking down the path towards the village.

'Ifan the bidder is on his way!' called Siôn. 'I saw him come down past the rock.'

'Are you sure it's him?' said Gwyneth.

'Who else would be wearing a top hat, you idiot, especially one decorated with ribbons and flowers?'

'Oh, I can see his white apron and his stick with the ribbons and flowers!' said Gwyneth, clapping her hands. 'It's definitely Ifan.'

Ifan's job was to invite everyone to the wedding. There were no postmen in those days and no one to deliver invitation cards. So people had to pay a man to go from house to house to spread the news – and to remind everyone to bring a wedding present!

Ifan never knocked on anyone's door. He just lifted the latch and walked in. He walked into Gwyneth's home, rapped the floor three times with his stick and made this speech.

'Friends, I have come to invite you to the wedding of Rhys and Meinir in the old church of Clynnog Fawr three weeks Saturday, on Midsummer Day. After the ceremony they will be returning to Meinir's house for a sumptuous meal. You are warmly invited to attend, but remember to bring a present. Anything will do – knives and forks, a cartload of potatoes, dishes, saucepans – anything! Thank you for your attention and good day to you!'

After Ifan had delivered the same message to every home in the valley, his work was done. But he wasn't quite so steady on his feet as he made his way back up the steep path. He'd had far too many glasses of home-brewed beer.

The three weeks flew by and soon it was the night before the wedding. On that night guests would bring their presents to the bride's house, especially if the present was large and bulky. No one wanted to turn up at the wedding with a sack of turnips!

Whenever possible, the gifts were displayed in the best room in the house, which was known simply as 'The Room'. Rhys and Meinir were given lots of presents that night – cheese, corn, potatoes, butter, dishes, cloth, furniture and lamps – and even pigs, hens, geese and calves, everything they needed to set up their own smallholding.

'Well, Rhys,' asked Siôn. 'Are you satisfied?'

'More than satisfied!' replied Rhys. 'I never realised people were so kind.'

'Neither did I,' said Meinir.

'Do you see what time it is?' said Siôn. 'It's half past ten. I don't suppose anyone else will come tonight and we have a long day ahead of us tomorrow.' He winked at Rhys.

'A very long day!' giggled Gwyneth. 'It won't be easy

getting Meinir to the church, I promise you. There'll be a few problems along the way.'

Everyone said goodnight and turned a blind eye when Rhys threw his arms around Meinir and kissed her.

It was the custom at that time to try and stop the bride reaching the church. Her friends and family would pretend she didn't want to marry and place all sorts of obstacles in her path. It added to the fun – and Gwyneth and her friends were determined to have as much fun as they possibly could!

*   *   *

Midsummer Day dawned. It was the morning of the wedding, a fine summer morning. The sun shone on Nant Gwrtheyrn, there were no clouds in the sky and the silken sea was as calm as a millpond. Not that Rhys and friends had time to appreciate it. They had all stayed the night in Rhys's house and had got up at the crack of dawn to go and find Meinir.

But Gwyneth had got there first!

'I can't open the door, Rhys,' said Siôn.

'That's strange,' replied Rhys. 'Mam and Dad never lock the door. Perhaps the wood has swollen after last week's rain. Give it a good tug.'

'You're a weakling, Siôn. You'll have to eat more porridge,' teased another of the lads.

Siôn kept pulling and pulling until Rhys realised that someone had tied the latch. In the end the young men had to climb out of the window because the back door had been tied up too.

There were other obstacles ahead. On the way to

Meinir's home, they came across a fallen tree, locked gates and, worst of all, a heap of carts. All the carts of the valley had been parked higgledy-piggledy at the entrance to the lane. By the time they'd cleared them away, it was a very muddy group of young men who rode up to the house. Even then they couldn't get through the door until the best man and the bridesmaid had taken part in a poetry contest.

From behind the door Gwyneth's voice rang out:

'Good morning to you, young men one and all.
What is your reason for paying this call?
If it's breakfast you're after, then you must beware.
The summer was poor and the pantry is bare.'

Siôn had to answer at once – and he did so with this poem:

'The man who sent us to you
Is loving and true.
He asks you with pride
For Meinir, his bride.'

The two young people swapped poem after poem and the men were only allowed in, when Gwyneth failed to answer quickly enough. To the surprise of Rhys and his friends the house was full of strangers. At least they looked strange. Everyone, including Meinir, was in disguise.

'Siôn, as you are the best man,' croaked an old man who was sitting in the corner, 'you must try and guess which one of us is Meinir. You have two minutes to do so and it won't be easy!' The old man began to laugh and it was only then that Siôn realised it was Gwyneth. No, his task would not be easy.

He studied each person in turn, but it was hopeless. All their faces had been carefully painted.

'Come on. You've already had a minute,' said Gwyneth. 'If you don't find Meinir before the time's up, you'll have to kiss me.'

'Oh no!' Siôn pretended to be terrified. 'Where are you Meinir? Where are you?' he quavered.

Everyone doubled up with laughter, especially Rhys who had recognised Meinir as soon as he walked into the house. Although she was dressed in her grandmother's clothes and made to look as old as the hills, he had recognised her laughing blue eyes. Of course he didn't want to spoil the fun, so he said nothing. Instead he watched Siôn plant a big kiss on Gwyneth's cheek which made her blush bright red.

'Right, off you go, you scamps,' said Gwyneth. 'We want to change. Go and wait for us out on the yard.'

Rhys and his friends waited on horseback. After ten minutes, they began to get suspicious. After quarter of an hour they realised all was not well. And they were right. From behind the house came a squeal of laughter and the sound of hoofs galloping away. Meinir and her friends had tricked them again.

'Come on, lads! They're trying to escape across the fields!' yelled Siôn.

'Yes, come on, or we'll never get to the church,' said Rhys.

'There they are! They're going towards the black rock!' shouted his friend. 'We'll catch them in no time!'

After a hard gallop they saw the girls head for Nant

42

Woods and thought the chase would soon be over. First they caught up with Gwyneth.

'Right, Gwyneth. We've got you,' panted Rhys. 'Where's Meinir?'

'I told her to hide in the woods for a while and then head for the church with you before it gets too late,' Gwyneth replied.

Although he was in a hurry to get to Clynnog, Rhys joined in the fun and went looking for Meinir. To his surprise there was no sign of her.

The minutes ticked by. After an hour the laughter had died away. The friends were afraid that something had gone badly wrong. Rhys and Siôn began to comb the woods, shouting to Meinir at the tops of their voices.

'Meinir! Meinir! Can you hear me?' shouted Rhys.

No one answered.

'Perhaps she doubled back to the pathway,' said Siôn.

'She can't have,' said Gwyneth. 'I saw her go into the woods.'

'Meinir! Meinir! Can you hear me?' shouted Rhys.

Still there was no answer.

They searched in vain all afternoon and, by evening, everyone in the valley knew that Meinir was missing. They all searched for her. Even after nightfall they kept on searching. Dozens of lanterns were seen flickering on the beach, the slopes of the Eifl and even on the black rock. They called her name and Rhys shouted louder than anyone.

'Meinir! Meinir! Where are you?'

To Siôn he said, 'I'm sure she's somewhere in the woods.'

'But Rhys,' Siôn replied, 'we've combed every inch of

the woods. She can't be here. Come home for a rest. We'll search again tomorrow.'

'No, I can't stop. Meinir must be here somewhere. I know it.'

And so they went on searching all night, but there was no sign of Meinir. It was as if she'd vanished from the face of the earth.

* * *

They searched and searched for two more days but found nothing. By this time Rhys had collapsed from exhaustion and so Gwyneth decided to visit a witch who lived on the slopes of the Eifl. Though her heart was in her mouth, she made her way determinedly towards the stone house that nestled in the heather.

'Edna Lwyd – are you there?' she called.

'Yes, Gwyneth.'

'H... how did you know my name?' Gwyneth stammered.

'Edna Lwyd knows many things.'

'Do you know where Meinir is?'

'Yes, I do.'

'Will someone find her?'

'Yes.'

'Will Rhys find her?'

'Yes.'

'When will that be?'

'When a light from the sky reveals her.'

'When will she come back?'

'She has never left . . . but I've had enough of your questions. Go now. I have spells to prepare. It's no use looking for her anyway. Only the light will show you where she is.'

The witch's message was so strange that Gwyneth didn't breathe a word to anyone. How could a light from the sky find Meinir?

After many days of searching, the people of the valley called a halt and returned to their work with heavy hearts. Something dreadful had happened to poor Meinir. But one man went on searching. Rhys could not give up. Though mad with despair he searched night after night and cried out her name.

The months went by. One wild night a thunderstorm rumbled round the rocks of the Eifl. Everyone huddled in their homes, everyone apart from poor Rhys who was scouring the slopes. As the storm drew closer, lightning flashed overhead. In the valley it was as bright as day and thunder drowned Rhys's voice as he cried for his Meinir.

As he reached Nant Woods, a flash of lightning dazzled him. It had struck an oak tree close by, the oldest and largest oak tree in the forest. It was from this very oak that William Cae'r Nant had cut the twigs to make the broom for Rhys and Meinir to jump over. On its bark, long before that, Rhys had carved a heart with both their initials inside.

Now the oak was split in two and, as another flash lit up the sky, Rhys realised he was looking at a skeleton trapped inside. It was the skeleton of Meinir in her wedding dress. She had hidden in the hollow oak tree and failed to free herself. The words of Edna Lwyd, the witch of the Eifl, had come true, but poor Rhys would never know that. He had died of shock when he realised his search was at an end.

*　　*　　*

That was a sad story, but Nant Gwrtheyrn is no longer a sad place. The houses that were once in ruins are now bright and bustling. It's a good place to visit. And if you go there you will find a restaurant called Caffi Meinir, or Meinir's Café – which proves that this story is true!

MARGED THE STRONG

Who is the strongest person in Wales? Could it be the wrestler El Bandito? El Bandito's real name is Orig Williams. He is as strong as a horse – or even two horses – and has travelled the world and wrestled with the strongest of men. On his travels El Bandito always wears a jacket with a Red Dragon design to show he's a Welshman.

There is no man in Wales who can beat El Bandito, let alone a woman. And yet, two and a half centuries ago, the strongest person in Wales was a woman. Her name was Marged, daughter of Ifan. There were many strong people at that time, so she must have been exceptional.

Many tales are still told about Marged. Here are some of them.

On a fine afternoon in late September a stranger was walking down towards the village of Drws-y-Coed in Snowdonia from the direction of Rhyd-ddu. On the outskirts of the village a man stepped out of a neat little cottage at the side of the road and the traveller stopped to chat to him.

'Good afternoon,' he said. 'Isn't it a lovely day?'

'It is indeed, sir,' the man replied. 'The weather has been kind to us, though I rarely get the chance to appreciate it.'

'Why is that?'

'I'm a miner. My job is to dig for copper in a mine called Owl's Chimney. We don't see much sun underground, I can tell you!'

'No, I'm sure you don't,' said the traveller.

'But tell me, what brings a stranger to this area?' the miner asked.

'Well, I've just walked up Snowdon,' the other explained, 'and from the top I spotted this valley. Gruffydd Roberts, who was my guide, told me of its connection with the story of Llew Llaw Gyffes, so I felt I had to come and visit it. But to tell you the truth, my friend . . . I'm sorry, I don't know your name.'

'Tomos Ifan, sir.'

'My name is Thomas too – Thomas Pennant. Well, to tell you the truth I feel rather tired. Walking up Snowdon is easier said than done. Is there anywhere I could stay the night?'

'There certainly is,' said Tomos Ifan. 'Can you hear the sound of a harp?'

'Yes. Where is it coming from?'

'It's coming from an inn called Y Telyrnia and if you're interested in stories, that's the place for you. The landlady is Marged, daughter of Ifan. She's the one who's playing the harp. I'm going there to wet my whistle and, if you like, I'll show you the way.'

Thomas Pennant thanked him kindly and, as the two of them headed for the inn, he remarked, 'So the landlady can play the harp?'

'She's an amazing character, Mr Pennant. Not only can she play the harp and sing, but she also composed the tune – and made the harp itself! The tune she's singing now is called Merch Megan. It's very popular in these parts.'

'My word, what a talented woman!' said Thomas Pennant. 'I'm so glad I came to Drws-y-coed!'

'Oh, you don't know the half of it,' replied Tomos Ifan. 'Marged can write poetry too. And she's a shoemaker and tailor!'

'Good heavens!'

'But hunting is her great delight. Can you hear the hounds barking and howling? That's because they can hear Marged's voice. She has scores of hunting dogs, including greyhounds, terriers and foxhounds. They tell me she's caught more foxes than all the other hunters in the county put together.'

'Well, let's go and see this amazing woman,' said Thomas Pennant excitedly. He had already spotted the sign Y Telyrnia hanging outside the inn and from inside came the sound of fiddles and voices and laughter.

When the traveller stepped into the inn and saw Marged, his eyes nearly popped out of his head. She was huge – well over six feet tall, with hair as black as a raven and hands like shovels! Tomos took him to meet her and Marged shook his hand warmly in between drawing pints of ale for her thirsty customers.

'My goodness, she's tall! And strong!' croaked Thomas Pennant, whose face was white as a sheet. 'She nearly crushed my fingers! I wouldn't like to pick a fight with her.'

'Nor me,' said Tomos. 'She's as strong as two of us miners put together, and we're all pretty strong. No weakling would last five days in that mine, I'm telling you. And yet I saw Marged throw six drunken miners out of the inn last week without any help at all from her husband.'

'So she's married, is she?'

'Yes, she is, but Richard Morris is nothing like his wife. There he is skulking in that corner over there.'

'That little man?' said Thomas Pennant in disbelief. 'He's not half the size of Marged.'

'Exactly. He's had his ears boxed several times by her and they say he only agreed to marry her, after she'd given him a good hiding. But they also say she thinks the world of him – which is just as well!'

Thomas Pennant spent a very entertaining evening in the inn, listening to Marged sing and hearing stories of her great strength. In the morning after a huge plateful of bacon and eggs, served by one of the most amazing characters in the whole of Wales, he continued his journey along the Nantlle Valley.

*   *   *

Some years later the copper mine at Drws-y-coed fell on hard times and many had to leave the area to look for work. Among them were Marged and Richard Morris, who went to live at Pen Llyn, near Cwm-y-glo, on the shores of Lake Padarn. Tomos Ifan moved to the same area and settled in Nant Peris. He'd had more than enough of the copper mine, and earned his living by guiding strangers to the summit of Snowdon.

He was weeding his garden one day, when he heard footsteps.

'Is there anyone at home?' called a voice.

'Yes. I'm in the back garden,' Tomos replied.

The footsteps came down the side path.

'Oh, there you are,' said the visitor. 'I need someone to guide me to the top of Snowdon. I have walked up to the top once before from the direction of Cwellyn lake . . .'

'I know that, Mr Pennant,' said Tomos, laying down his hoe.

'What did you say? How do you know my name?' asked the visitor in astonishment.

'I'm Tomos Ifan, sir. Do you remember staying at Y Telyrnia some years ago.'

'Well, of course I do!' cried Thomas Pennant. 'I'm so pleased to meet you again, Tomos. I didn't recognise you with that beard. So you've left the darkness behind you? I'm sure you're making the most of the sunshine.'

'I am indeed,' Tomos replied.

'Tell me, what happened to that remarkable woman, Marged?' asked Thomas Pennant. 'Is she still living in Drws-y-Coed?'

'No, she isn't. You passed her house on the way here today. She's been living in Pen Llyn for some years.'

'Does she keep an inn?' asked the visitor hopefully. 'I'm looking for a place to stay tonight and I wouldn't mind hearing her sing again.'

'No, I'm afraid she no longer keeps an inn,' laughed Tomos Ifan. 'She rows the boats that carry the copper from Snowdon along Padarn and Peris lakes.'

'She rows a boat?' said Thomas Pennant. 'Why on earth does she do that?'

'Because there isn't a proper road from Llanberis Pass to Pen Llyn,' said Tomos. 'There's only a track and so the copper has to be brought down in special boats. It's awfully hard work.'

'Well, I'm sure Marged can cope,' said Thomas Pennant, who still treasured the memory of the huge woman he had met at the inn. 'She's a giant, isn't she? Does her husband Richard help her by any chance?'

'What do you think?' chuckled Tomos. 'He wouldn't be much use on a boat! Marged's got another woman helping her.'

'What? Another strong woman!' cried Thomas Pennant. 'There must be something in the water round here to make them so tough!'

'I don't know about that. But I do know that Myfanwy is amazingly strong. By the way . . .' – Tomos's eyes twinkled – 'Marged built the boat herself.'

'Is there anything that woman can't do?' gasped the visitor.

'Probably not. Well, Mr Pennant, shall we meet at Ceunant Mawr tomorrow morning at half past eight and start our journey there? The weather is calm and settled, so we can make our way down to Gorffwysfa Peris at the top of the Pass and then walk home past the lakes. And with luck you'll meet Marged, sweet daughter of Ifan, once again.'

'I do hope so, Tomos! I'll see you tomorrow!'

*   *   *

Next morning Thomas Pennant was ready and waiting for his guide at the foot of Snowdon. At exactly half past eight the two of them set off for the summit with Tomos pointing out places of interest along the way.

Thomas Pennant enjoyed listening to his stories, especially when he talked about the Snowdon copper mines and the miners who, to save walking up and down each day, lived in small cottages, called barracks, tucked away on the slopes.

'And this is the copper that Marged carries in her boat?' asked the traveller, as they walked up the mountain.

'Yes, and the copper from the Nant Peris mine. The copper's taken down by mules and loaded into flat-bottomed boats that can carry huge loads – especially if they're rowed by two such excellent rowers as Marged and Myfanwy.'

'Tell me more about Marged,' urged Thomas Pennant. 'She's such a fascinating woman, I'd like to write a book about her one day.'

'Well,' said Tomos, 'she's still a good huntress, though she doesn't ride out as often as she did when she was at the inn. She works very hard now, so she hasn't much spare time.'

'Oh, I do hope we see her at work this afternoon,' said his companion.

'We should do,' Tomos replied. 'Until recently Marged would have taken a gentleman like you for a ride in her boat, but I'm afraid there's no chance of that now.'

'Why is that?'

'Well, some big oaf got hold of her in the middle of the lake and tried to steal a kiss or some such nonsense. And do you know what she did?'

'No.'

'She lifted him up by the strap of his bag and told him she'd drop him in the lake if he didn't promise to behave. The man couldn't swim, so he didn't have much choice. Oh, I had such fun that day when I heard him shouting and begging to be put back in the boat and rowed ashore.'

'So I take it Marged's as strong as ever?' chuckled Thomas Pennant.

'Strong? You bet she is. She can straighten horseshoes with her bare hands and she wrestles regularly.'

'Wrestles, did you say?'

'Yes. Wrestling matches are very popular round here and Marged is always challenging the lads. Not one of them has managed to beat her yet!'

And so the day went by, with the two men chatting away and swapping stories. Thomas Pennant had a whale of a time and saw many astonishing sights, including the grave of a giant, the valley where Arthur fought his last battle, the rocks that guard the cave where he and his soldiers lie asleep and a lake where a monster lives.

At the end of the afternoon, the two of them walked down past the copper mines to Eisteddfa Peris at the top of Llanberis Pass. On the way they saw the Cromlech of

Gathrig Bwt and Tomos told the story of the witch who used to live beneath the stone. She used to eat children till a brave man cut her head off.

'Ugh!' said Thomas Pennant. 'And you're telling me she lived under the cromlech by the side of this path?'

'Yes, till a man from Llanberis finished her off with a sickle.'

The two walked on till they came within sight of Lake Peris.

'Look, there's the lake,' said Tomos. 'If Marged's out rowing today, you two can meet up again.'

That put a spring in Thomas's step and soon the two of them had reached the shores of the lake. There they met a man loading copper into a boat.

'Good afternoon,' said Thomas Pennant to the boatman.

'And good afternoon to you too, sir,' he replied. 'Can I help you?'

'I hope so. Is Marged around today? I'd like to meet her.'

'I'm afraid not. She's gone off hunting on the slopes of Elidir.'

'Oh, what a shame!' cried Thomas Pennant. 'I take it you know her well?'

'Yes, everyone who rows on this lake knows Marged. She's just had a new terrier and they've gone off hunting foxes. The terrier had better be a good one, if it's to match old Ianto.'

'Ianto?' said Thomas Pennant. 'Who is he?'

'Ianto was Marged's favourite terrier. He was only a tiny little thing, but as brave as a lion.'

'What happened to him?' asked Tomos.

'He was always in the boat with Marged, but one day he picked up a scent and followed it for hours on end. By the time he came to a house, the little dog was absolutely starving. The door was open and there was a juicy joint of meat on the table, so Ianto jumped up and ate it all. Unfortunately he was caught by the owner, a huge miner called Jac. In his temper Jac killed Ianto with his bare hands and threw the body into the river.'

'Poor little thing,' said Tomos.

'Yes, but that isn't the end of the story. When Marged heard what had happened, off she rushed to Jac's house. No one else would have dared, because he's a big hulk of a man. Jac had finished work and was having a wash when Marged arrived and demanded to talk to him. Jac said he was busy and Marged offered to come back later on.

'"Huh! What for?" grunted Jac.

'Well, Marged did go back and she offered to pay four times the value of the meat that Ianto had eaten, as long as Jac paid her for Ianto.

'"Go and take a running jump!" replied Jac. "Off you go before I throw you into the river!'

'Marged said nothing, but took aim with her fist and flattened him. If she'd hit him again, he'd have been stone dead. Luckily she didn't. She just searched his pockets and took out enough money to pay for another dog. And that's why you've missed her today. She's out hunting with her new dog.'

*   *   *

The new dog brought Marged great joy. He was a fine

hunting dog. In fact he was every bit as good as Ianto and was a favourite of hers for many years. But, though Marged was happy, Thomas Pennant went home a disappointed man. He never did meet Marged again. Some years later he wrote a book about his journeys through Wales. In it he describes Marged and her amazing strength and says how much he regretted not meeting her that day in Llanberis.

They say that Marged lived till she was a hundred and two and never had a day's illness. She was still wrestling when she was well over seventy, and no one could beat her. She was quite a lady!

Marged and El Bandito would have made a brilliant tag team, don't you think? They'd have been champions of the world and the Red Dragon would be flying high!

TWM SIÔN CATI

In Ystrad-ffin this year
Bold men cry out in fear.
The rocks themselves are wet with sweat,
For Twm Siôn Cati's near!

If you lived in Carmarthenshire or Ceredigion four hundred years ago, you'd have heard lots of poems about Twm Siôn Cati. But who was he and why was he so terrifying? Well, Twm wasn't terrifying at all – except to those who took advantage of ordinary people. He was a Welsh Robin Hood, who robbed the rich and gave to the poor. He was a clever fellow too who knew the country like the back of his hand and was familiar with the history of every hill and dale. Though he was very mischievous, he was also a gentleman who was ready to help his neighbours out of difficulty. No wonder the country people thought the world of him and still remember him today. Shall I tell you about him?

* * *

Let's start off with his name – Twm Siôn Cati. How did he end up with such a strange name? Well, Twm, which is short for Thomas, was his own Christian name. Siôn, which is Welsh for John, was the name of his father, Sir John Wynn of Gwydir near Llanrwst in North Wales. Sir John was rich, but also very cruel. He was the sort of person whom Twm would rob later on in his life. Twm's third name, Cati, came from his mother Catrin, who was known as Cati to her friends. So there we have it: Twm Siôn Cati.

Twm was brought up in a house called Porth y Ffynnon near Tregaron in Ceredigion. Later the house became known as Twm Siôn Cati's Palace, but that was after Twm became famous and before he had to escape to a cave! Twm was very happy in Porth y Ffynnon. There he learnt how to play all sorts of mischievous tricks on his neighbours, but he also learnt a lot about the history of the area and of Wales itself. That was what made him determined not to follow his father's example. He wanted to help the poor, not steal their land.

One day, soon after leaving school, Twm saw an old lady walking past his home in the direction of Tregaron.

'Good afternoon, Lizzie Pugh,' he called. 'It's a fine day.'

'Yes indeed, Twm my boy,' the old lady replied. 'But

I'm sorry I can't stop and talk to you. I've got to hurry along to the market to buy a new cooking pot from Smith's stall. I can't really afford a new one, because the rent is so high and the hens aren't laying, but the old one's worn through. So you see, I've no choice but to go and buy from that old rogue even though he asks ridiculous prices for his pots and pans.'

'Does he indeed?' said Twm with a thoughtful glint in his eye. 'May I come with you to Tregaron, Lizzie?'

'Of course, my boy,' replied Lizzie at once. 'What made you change your mind so suddenly?'

'I want to help you carry the pot home,' said Twm. 'And perhaps I can help you in some other way too.'

'Thank you for being so kind to an old lady,' said Lizzie and off they both went to Tregaron.

When they reached Smith's stall, Twm went straight to the owner and asked the price of the cooking pots. They were far too expensive, just as Lizzie had said.

'You should be ashamed of yourself!' said Twm. 'How can you ask such a high price for a pot with a hole in it?'

'A hole?' snapped Smith. 'There aren't any holes in my pots. Every one of them is brand new.'

'I tell you what,' said Twm. 'If I can show you a pot with a hole in it, will you give it to me for nothing?'

'Of course,' the man replied. 'It'll be no good to anyone if it's got a hole in it.'

'Right. There's a hole in this one,' said Twm, picking up the biggest pot in the shop.

'Where? I can't see a hole!'

'Stick your head inside and you'll soon see it,' said Twm.

'Give it here,' grunted Smith. He snatched the pot and

poked his head inside. 'I can't see a hole. You're making it up, boy!'

'Am I really? Well, if there's no hole, how did you manage to get your head inside?' said Twm. And with that he picked up the pot and carried it off. Lizzie was delighted. Twm had got her an excellent pot and she hadn't had to pay a single penny!

From then on, there was no stopping Twm. He was the champion of the poor and soon people were flocking to him to ask for help.

One day there was a knock at the door. His mother answered.

'Hello, Cati,' said a voice.

'Oh, it's you, Daniel Prydderch,' replied Twm's mother. 'Come inside.'

'Is Twm in?'

'Yes,' called Twm. 'What can I do for you, Daniel?'

'On Saturday my wife Mari bought some cloth in the market to make winter clothes for the children,' said Daniel. 'We can't afford to buy ready-made clothes, you see. Well, to cut a long story short, she paid for four yards of cloth, but when she got home she found that the woman on the stall had only given her two yards.'

'Didn't she go back and complain?' asked Cati.

'Yes of course she did, but the stall-holder denies everything and insists that Mari only paid for two yards. I'm only a poor farm hand, as you know Twm, and I can't afford to lose that much money. Can you help me?'

'Of course I can, Daniel. What colour cloth was it?'

'Dark blue.'

'Right. You leave everything to me.'

The following Saturday Twm got to the market bright

and early and went straight to the cloth stall. While the cheating stall-holder was busy serving a customer, Twm checked to see if there was any of the dark blue cloth left. There was, so he quickly took hold of one end and wrapped the cloth round himself, spinning like a top as he did so. Then he walked off boldly to the next stall.

When the woman had finished serving, she realised some of her cloth was missing and went to look for it. She soon spotted Twm in his dark blue 'suit'. She was about to run after to him, when Twm turned round and walked up to her.

'I saw it all with my own eyes,' he said before the woman had a chance to say a word.

'What do you mean?' asked the stall-holder suspiciously.

'I saw the thief make off with your cloth. Tregaron is a terrible place. You can't trust anyone. I have to wrap my cloth around me like this so no one will steal it. Good day to you!' And off he went.

That day Mari Prydderch had enough cloth to make two suits for each of her children and the cheating stall-holder was taught a lesson, thanks to Twm Siôn Cati.

*   *   *

Twm had no mercy on the rich, so it was no surprise that in the end he was forced to flee from Porth y Ffynnon. He'd heard that officers of the law were looking for him and rather than be thrown into Cardigan jail he ran away. Like many a hero before him, he had to live in cave. This cave can still be seen near Ystradffin in Carmarthenshire.

Despite living in a cave, Twm was still a threat to his enemies. In fact he grew bolder and bolder. Now that he had such a fine hiding place, he decided to become a highwayman, though unlike other highwaymen he gave all his money to the poor and the needy.

Soon rich gentlemen were afraid to ride out on horseback and their wives were afraid to venture forth in their fine coaches. If they did, Twm the highwayman would gallop out of the trees and demand their money and all their jewels and gold rings. Despite cursing him roundly, they said he was a very polite highwayman – though he was cheeky enough to demand a kiss or even a dance from a pretty girl.

But then another highwayman turned up on Twm's patch. He was nothing like Twm. This one stole from everybody. He was rough and cruel and kept all the booty for himself. He was hated by rich and poor alike and especially by Twm Siôn Cati. So Twm decided to teach him a lesson.

Although Twm lived in a cave, it was quite a comfortable cave because he stored all his belongings there, including his clothes. One day Twm put on his best tweed suit, his white silk shirt, his leather shoes with silver buckles and, to top it all, a fine hat with a huge red feather.

He left his sword in the cave and rode off towards Rhandir-mwyn. Anyone would have taken him for a rich businessman or a wealthy drover returning home from a lucrative trip over the border.

'Stop right there!' The voice came from a small clump of trees at the side of the road.

'Whoa, Bess!' called Twm to his horse.

A highwayman stepped out, gun in hand. The gun was pointed directly at Twm's heart.

'On your way home, friend?' he asked.

'Y...yes,' squeaked Twm, trembling from head to foot. 'W...w...who are you? Are you that terrible Twm Siôn Cati?'

'Twm Siôn Cati – huh!' spat the intruder. 'I'm Black Dafydd and for your information, matey, I'm a highwayman too.'

'Oh, no!' screeched Twm. 'You're the famous Dafydd. What shall I do?'

'I'll tell you now,' Dafydd replied. 'You've got a fat purse in the pocket of that coat by the looks of it.'

'Yes, but...'

'Save your breath, man. I want that purse. Hand it over!'

'Here it is!' said Twm and he threw the purse over the hedge.

'You'll pay for this, you scum!' shouted Dafydd as he ran after it.

'We'll see about that,' murmured Twm, spurring his horse towards the woods. By the time the thief had retrieved the purse, Twm was galloping away on his own horse and leading Dafydd's by the rein. Dafydd cursed the 'gentleman' roundly for stealing his horse and a whole week's pickings, but at least he had a good fat purse to keep him going. Well, he thought he did, till he opened the purse and found it was full of nails!

*   *   *

Though Twm Siôn Cati had many brushes with the law

and the nobility, he never lost his freedom. But he did lose his heart – to a pretty girl.

One day Twm held up a very grand coach. When he saw it belonged to the mansion of Ystradffin, he thought he was in for a rich haul. The squire of Ystradffin was famous for two things: wealth and a cruel heart.

'Right, squire,' said Twm. 'Out you come. I'm asking for a contribution towards a good cause . . .'

Twm stopped open-mouthed. The most beautiful girl he'd ever seen had stepped out of the coach.

'You're not the squire!'

'No, and you're not collecting for charity,' she replied pertly.

'Who are you?'

'Elen Wyn, the squire's daughter, if you must know. And who are you?'

'Twm Siôn Cati.'

'Oh, so you are the Twm Siôn Cati my father's always cursing high and low,' said Elen with a mischievous smile.

Twm was so dazzled by Elen's beauty, he forgot to rob her of her jewels. Instead he let her go. Twm had fallen head over heels in love with the beautiful heiress of Ystradffin.

Luckily for Twm, Elen had fallen in love with him too. But unluckily for them both, the squire was after Twm's blood. Twm and Elen began to meet secretly behind her father's back. When the squire found out, he was beside himself.

'But I love Twm and want to marry him, father,' said Elen.

'Marry him! If I have half a chance, I'll fling the rogue

into the nearest jail – and throw the key away.'

When Twm heard this, he realised he had to get the better of the squire and it wasn't long before he had thought of a plan.

One night the squire heard a knock at his door. Standing there was a man in a long black cloak.

'Yes. What do you want?' he asked.

'I have come on behalf of Twm Siôn Cati, sir,' the stranger replied.

'What? He's got a nerve!'

'He's asking if he can see Elen for one last time.'

'One last time did you say?'

'Yes, sir. Once he's seen her, he promises to go back to live in North Wales.'

'Back to North Wales? I don't trust the rogue. What if he takes Elen with him?'

'He promises not to take her against her will, sir. Will you let her open the window and shake hands with him for one last time?'

'And if I do, does he promise to leave Ystradffin for ever?'

'Yes.'

'How can you be so sure? Who are you?'

'His servant, sir.'

'Right, if that's the only way to get rid of the rascal, I agree. Come back in five minutes and stand outside the parlour window.'

Five minutes later the parlour window opened and Elen's hand appeared. Someone took hold of it and kissed it gently.

'Twm, is that you?' whispered Elen.

'Yes, it's me. Open the curtains and see who else is here.'

Elen opened the curtains. When Twm's 'servant' took off his cloak, she realised it was the local vicar. Daniel and Mari Prydderch were there too, standing proudly beside Twm.

'Will you marry me, Elen?'

'Of course I will.'

They were married there and then. Within seconds the vicar had conducted the ceremony, Twm had placed the ring on Elen's finger and Daniel and Mari were witnesses. The squire could do nothing. After all he had promised Twm his daughter's hand!

*　　*　　*

Twm kept his word and left the area taking Elen with him. No one knows exactly where they went, but wherever it was, you can be sure they were as happy as could be.

Ystradffin is a fairly remote place and if you go there today, you will find little to remind you of Twm Siôn Cati, apart from the cave in the rocks near the village. Mind you, you wouldn't expect Twm to leave many clues behind. He wouldn't have been a successful highwayman if that had been the case.

The most important memorial to Twm is the respect the people of the area still have for him as the champion of poor country folk. That is why these tales are still told. See if you can find more stories about Twm Siôn Cati.

JEMIMA'S ARMY

In Wales we have many stories of heroes who defended their country with great bravery. Amongst them are Arthur, Llywelyn the Great, Llywelyn the Last and Owain Glyndwr. Though the list of heroines is far shorter, it does include such notable names as Gwenllian and Jemima Nicholas.

Two hundred years ago Jemima saved Wales from being overrun by the French when they invaded Pembrokeshire. Not only did she scupper the French, but she did so with the help of a group of women when the local soldiers had fled for their lives! Would you like to hear the story? I'm sure you would . . .

*　　*　　*

Jemima was the wife of a poor fisherman from Pencaer near Fishguard in Pembrokeshire. Before 1797 she was unknown outside her locality. Her neighbours knew her as a huge woman, over six feet tall, who worked as a cobbler. After the French had landed, she became famous throughout the land and poets sang her praises as they wandered from fair to fair.

Jemima was a woman who always stood up for her rights. She was not afraid of anyone or anything. One day a fishmonger underpaid Robat, her husband, for a catch of mackerel. When Jemima heard of it, she marched straight to the shop in Fishguard and harangued the owner in rich and colourful language. In the end the fishmonger was only too glad to pay up just to get rid of her!

Two hundred years ago Fishguard was a quiet little place on the shores of Cardigan Bay. There was little to worry the townspeople, as long as there were plenty of fish in the sea and the harvest was good. But when France declared war on Britain, the mood changed. There were fears that a French army would land in Wales and, to protect the country from invasion, a number of forts were built along the coastline at places such as Belan near Aber Menai in the north and Fishguard in the south. Huge guns and specially trained soldiers were stationed there.

The sight of these forts made everyone feel very uneasy and in the summer of 1796 all sorts of rumours were rife. There was talk of French spies prowling the countryside. One 'spy' was hanged in England, when his ship was wrecked on the beach. It was only after the poor creature was dead, that people realised he wasn't a spy at all, but a monkey!

'I'll give those Frenchmen what for!' growled Jemima when she heard the rumours. 'If they so much as set foot in Pembrokeshire, they'll be sorry!'

'Quite right too!' said Robat, secretly thanking his lucky stars that his roots were deep in the soil of Pencaer.

'Well, you be careful when you're out at sea, Robat, in case those French rapscallions get hold of you. They're terrible people. They say they eat snails for dinner every day! Ugh!'

'We'll be perfectly safe, Jemima. Thomas Knox and his soldiers will defend us from the fort at Fishguard.'

'Thomas Knox, indeed!' scoffed Jemima. 'What does he know about fighting? He's a spoilt pup who's been pampered by his dad. All he does is strut around town in his soldier's uniform. If he sees a Frenchman coming, he'll run a mile, I'm telling you.'

Little did Robat know how right she was.

*　　*　　*

Autumn and winter went by without any sign of the Frenchmen. By the beginning of 1797 most Pembrokeshire people had forgotten all about the threat of invasion. The weather was too stormy and the sea too rough for ships to sail close to shore and in any case everyone was too busy having a good time. Robat and Jemima Nicholas and their neighbours celebrated the traditional New Year's feast of Hen Galan on the twelfth of January, brewed ale and generally enjoyed themselves. The last thing on their mind was an attack by Frenchmen.

The French were well aware of that and so an army of

one and a half thousand men was secretly preparing to sail for Wales in four ships. These men were the worst kind of ruffians, many of whom had newly been released from jail. All they needed was fine weather and a calm sea. In February 1797 they saw their chance, weighed anchor and sailed for Wales.

The ships sailed boldly past Cornwall and headed for Pembrokeshire under the very noses of the British navy. They had hoisted Union Jacks to the tops of their masts, so no one would suspect them. It never crossed the minds of the British sailors that a foreign ship would dare to fly the Union Jack.

Well, the French may have fooled the British navy, but they did not fool the people of Pembrokeshire. By February the twenty-second, when the ships were sailing close to St. Davids, they were spotted by Tomos Williams of Trelethin. Tomos was an old retired sailor and, because he had the sea in his blood, he knew at once that the ships belonged to the French.

He sent an urgent message to the authorities in St Davids, while continuing to watch the ships. It was clear to him that they were looking for a suitable landing place and by the afternoon they were making for Carreg Wastad on the Pencaer peninsula near Fishguard. Within a few hours the invading army had set foot on the soil of Pembrokeshire and the local people were scared out of their wits – all except Jemima Nicholas.

'Just look at them, Robat,' she said. 'They've lit fires near Llanwnda. And what are they burning? Firewood that belongs to the good people of Pencaer, no doubt. Or even their furniture! Those rogues are capable of anything. For two pins I'd go and give them a hiding.'

'Give them a hiding?' wailed Robat. 'Are you mad, my dear? There are hundreds and hundreds of them. They'll either eat you alive or shoot you dead!'

'I doubt it! They wouldn't dare!'

'Maybe not, but you leave everything to Thomas Knox and his soldiers. They're the ones who'll defend us from the French. It's their job after all.'

'Huh! You and your Thomas Knox,' sniffed Jemima. 'He and his pretend soldiers couldn't frighten next door's cat, let alone drive away the Frenchmen with their tails between their legs.'

'Oh, be fair now, Jemima.'

'I am being fair! Knox and his gang are just playing at being soldiers. They're the ones who'll turn tail and run, you wait and see.'

*　　*　　*

The French landing had caused great panic in that corner of Pembrokeshire. The news spread like wildfire and most of the people of Pencaer fled to Fishguard, taking with them as many of their possessions as they could carry. They would have been even more terrified if they'd seen what was happening in the fort at the harbour mouth and heard the conversation between Knox and a soldier called Jones.

'Lieutenant, sir!' said Jones. 'We should be out at Pencaer defending the local people and their belongings.'

'That's enough, Jones!' sniffed Knox with a wave of his hand. 'Our duty is to stay here in the fort and defend the people of Fishguard. That's why my dear father built the fort and gave you such a splendid uniform to wear.'

'But sir, the French have landed in Pencaer!'

'Tut tut! I haven't seen hide nor hair of the blighters. It's just the local people making up silly stories.'

'You should have called at Carreg Wastad on your way here tonight,' insisted Jones. 'I have family in Pencaer and when my cousin Reuben tells me there are Frenchmen on Carreg Wastad, I know he's not joking!'

'I don't believe anything of the kind. I think your cousin's been drinking home brew and seeing things. No, we'll stay here tonight.'

'Sir, I've seen the Frenchmen!' called another soldier.

'So have I!'

'There are thousands of them round Carreg Wastad.'

'Well, you could be right,' conceded Knox. There was no point in denying the presence of the Frenchmen on the very land he should have been defending, but that didn't mean he was going to rush out to do his duty by the people of Pembrokeshire. 'Oh dear,' he sighed. 'It's dark. There's no moon, so we won't be able to spot these ruffians. Nothing for it but to wait till morning.'

So the doors of the fort were locked and, if the Frenchmen had only known it, they could have taken Fishguard that night as easy as pie.

But the Frenchmen had other things on their mind. After their long voyage, and after many of them had had to survive on prison food for months on end, they were busy feasting on the eggs, cheese, bacon, chickens, geese and ducks that they'd stolen from the people of the area. It was the best food many of them had ever eaten. And there was drink as well. They found casks of smuggled beer, wine and brandy in some of the houses, so by midnight most of the invaders were too drunk to move.

Even Knox and his pretend soldiers could have defeated the French that night, if only they'd known.

*　　*　　*

Though neither the French nor the soldiers stirred on that February night, the local people were on the move. By morning hundreds of them were flocking to Fishguard armed with pitchforks, axes, scythes and any sharp tool they could lay their hands on. In their midst was Jemima.

'We must throw these rotten Frenchmen back into the sea!' she roared.

'But how?' asked her neighbour. 'They've all got guns and we only have farm tools.'

'I know. That doesn't help,' admitted Jemima. 'But Knox's soldiers have guns and they're not doing anything. Their leader's scared of his own shadow and is holed up in his fort. We'll just have to march to Pencaer and do his work for him.'

'But Jemima,' the man objected, 'the French will shoot anything that moves. A gang of them went to Brestgarn farm last night and when the grandfather clock struck the hour, they had such a fright, they shot it! They thought someone was hiding inside!'

'What we really need is a troop of redcoats to scare the life out of them,' said another neighbour.

'Exactly,' said Jemima. 'And I know how we can get hold of them.'

'But there aren't any redcoats in Fishguard!'

'No redcoats in Fishguard!' said Jemima. 'Of course

there are. Can't you see them?'

'No! Where are they?'

'What am I wearing?' said Jemima. 'And all the other women too? We're wearing red woollen shawls.'

'Yes. So?'

'Well, from a distance they'll look exactly like the red coats of soldiers. If I can get enough women to come with me to Pencaer, we'll give those Frenchmen a scare. How about it, girls?'

The women roared their support for Jemima and off they went towards the French camp with their menfolk following at a distance.

On the way they saw a dozen Frenchmen keeping watch in a field above Fishguard. How could the women creep past without alerting them?

'Leave it to me,' said Jemima. She sneaked along the hedge that bordered the field, then, with a bloodcurdling roar, she jumped through a gap and ran at the Frenchmen with sparks flying from the metal soles of her clogs. In her hand was a huge pitchfork.

'Mon Dieu! The Devil has come to get us! Run!' wailed a Frenchman.

'Don't you dare or I'll stick this pitchfork in a very tender place and you won't be able to sit down for a month!'

'Sacrebleu! The devil can speak Welsh!'

'And he's dressed like a woman!'

'Come on! Put your hands up! Now! No nonsense!' said Jemima.

At once the twelve men raised their hands in terror. They were marched to Fishguard and put under lock and key. They didn't mind where they were as long as

they were safe from Jemima.

Jemima and her army of women walked on towards Llanwnda and Carreg Wastad. On the way they heard noises in a cowshed and Jemima insisted on going in. After a moment's silence, followed by terrified shouts, the door of the cowshed was thrown open and out came Jemima with a Frenchman under each arm!

'These two ruffians were snoring in the cowshed surrounded by empty bottles,' she said. 'Take them to the others. It shouldn't take us long to capture the lot of them.'

But the women knew they were risking their lives as they approached Trehywel farm where the French had set up their headquarters. If the Frenchmen saw through their trick and realised they didn't have a gun between them, it would be the end of them. They would stand no chance against one and a half thousand armed men.

'Look,' said Jemima. 'The French ships have sailed away. These men have been caught like rats in a trap. If we can trick them into thinking they're surrounded by hundreds of soldiers, they'll lose heart and give up.'

'What do you want us to do then, Jemima?'

'We'll march slowly in a long line over the hill towards Trehywel with our pitchforks and scythes resting like guns on our shoulders. The Frenchmen will think we're a huge army.'

And that is exactly what the women did. Though it took courage to march within sight of the French who were milling below, it was clear within seconds that Jemima's plan had worked. The enemy started running around in a panic.

'Hooray! We've fooled them!'

'Yes, but don't move!' said Jemima. 'If we stand our ground and don't go too close, they may lay down their arms without a fight.'

That night two of the Frenchmen sneaked through the lines of 'soldiers' who surrounded them. Jemima had spotted them, but did not stand in their way because she guessed they were bringing a message of surrender from the French army. Ironically this letter was addressed to Thomas Knox, who had done absolutely nothing to repel the invaders!

But by that time the real soldiers had arrived and they were the ones who arranged for the French to lay down their arms on Goodwick beach the next day. As you can imagine, they were astonished to find that the French had surrendered without firing a single bullet – except the one that had hit the clock! But they weren't half as astonished as the Frenchmen, who were horrified to find they'd been tricked by Jemima and an 'army' of women who didn't have a single gun between them. But by that time there was nothing they could do and so Jemima became a heroine, not only to the people of Pembrokeshire but to the whole of Wales.

* * *

If you go to Fishguard and Pencaer, you will see many reminders of the French invasion. There is a painting of Thomas Knox's so-called soldiers on the wall outside the Royal Oak inn in Fishguard and in nearby Goodwick a stone marks the spot where the Frenchmen surrendered on the 24th of February 1797. There is another stone at Carreg Wastad to mark the spot where they landed. The grandfather's clock still has pride of place in Brestgarn and though it has a bullet hole in its case, it keeps time perfectly! If you visit the graveyard of St Mary's Church Fishguard, you will see the grave of Jemima Nicholas, and if you're hungry after your visit, why not call in Caffi Jemeima in town? I wonder if it serves French fries?

GWENLLIAN'S FIELD

In Carmarthenshire, in the shadow of the mountain called Mynydd y Garreg, near the town and castle of Kidwelly, stands a farm called Maes Gwenllian, or Gwenllian's Field. Today the farm is divided into many fields, but centuries ago there was only one large field. Why is it called Gwenllian's Field? Who was Gwenllian? And why was her field so special?

Well, the name bears witness to a remarkable story, the story of Gwenllian, one of the bravest of Welsh women, who lived eight hundred and fifty years ago. Long after she died Rhydderch the Storyteller would entertain the court of Llywelyn the Great, prince of Wales, with the tale of Gwenllian. Let's travel back in time and listen to his story.

*   *   *

It was a cold January night and at his court in Abergwyngregyn in Arfon Llywelyn and a gathering of friends from all over Wales had just enjoyed a fine banquet. Venison was the main dish, because Llywelyn, accompanied by his guests and his faithful dog Gelert, had been hunting that day in the forests of Snowdonia. Now they were all sitting in front of a roaring fire in the great hall of the palace.

'Rhydderch!'

'Yes, my prince?'

'Have you a good story to while away the hours before bedtime?'

'I do, my Lord, and as many of your guests have come from the south, I shall tell the tale of a brave heroine who came from that part of the country. She was one of your ancestors, Llywelyn.'

'Was she really?' said the prince. 'What was her name?'

'Gwenllian. She was the daughter of Gruffudd ap Cynan, your great-grandfather, who used to live in the palace of Aberffraw before your time.'

A smile spread across Llywelyn's face. He had heard such a lot about his famous great-grandfather. He sat back on his splendid throne with his right hand resting on Gelert's head. The dog appeared to be smiling too. They both knew they were in for a good story.

'Gwenllian was a beautiful young woman,' began Rhydderch. 'The long hair that flowed down her back was as bright as the sun in May. Her skin was white as snow and her cheeks as red as apples in autumn.

'Everyone from the tip of Anglesey to the farthest corner of Gwent had fallen in love with the lovely Gwenllian, princess of Snowdonia. She in turn had fallen in love with a brave young prince called Gruffudd ap Rhys who came from Deheubarth in the south-west. At their marriage North and South were united in joy, and the young people themselves were as happy as could be.

'Sad to say, their happiness did not last. Then, as now, the Normans prowled the land and at the least opportunity would trample the local people underfoot. Gruffudd and Gwenllian, who had gone to live in Gruffudd's family home in Dinefwr near Llandeilo, always had to be on their guard against Norman treachery.

'Their greatest enemy was a man called Maurice de Londres. He was a devil in human shape. He was cruel to his own men and crueller still to the Welsh. He'd built himself an enormous castle in Kidwelly, on Gruffudd's land, and it was obvious to everyone that his plan was to do away with Gruffudd and steal all his property.

'Maurice really was the most evil of men. He would punish the Welsh at the least excuse. And if there was no excuse, he'd make one up.

'On the slopes of Mynydd y Garreg, above Maurice's castle, lived a huge man called Gronw, who had a beard the colour of autumn leaves. Gronw was a blacksmith and whenever he was hammering a horseshoe on his anvil, he would sing happily and his voice would echo for miles and miles. He was a kind-hearted fellow, but that didn't stop Maurice capturing him and dragging him back to his castle on the excuse that he might make swords and daggers for the Welshmen. Maurice hated the Welsh and was always trying to get the better of them.

'But Maurice wasn't the only one. All over Wales at that time the Normans were looking for ways to trample the Welsh underfoot. They'd already defeated England, but had yet to conquer Wales.'

'And they still haven't managed it!' roared Llywelyn the Great.

'And they never will while we're alive!' shouted his men.

'In the end the Welsh had had enough of the tricks and cruelty of the Normans,' went on the storyteller. 'Gwynedd and Dyfed rose against the enemy and only the bravest – or stupidest – of Normans remained in those parts. The others fled over Offa's Dyke.

'When Gruffudd heard news of the fighting in the north, he went at once to help his father-in-law drive out the enemy. He took an army of men with him and left Gwenllian and their two eldest sons to defend the castle with the aid of a small band of soldiers.

'Gruffudd's plan was to return home with the army of the North and together they would drive the Normans from his land and destroy Kidwelly Castle once and for all. But while he was away, another army of Normans landed in Carmarthen Bay. Now Maurice de Londres was a greater threat than ever – and the prince was away from home.

'But Gwenllian was a princess in her own right and was used to leading her people. After all she was the daughter of Gruffudd ap Cynan, a clever, impetuous and powerful man who came from the west. She was not prepared to stay in her castle and watch the Normans steal Welshmen's lands.

'Bravely the princess gathered her small band of soldiers. The local people joined them, armed with knives, spears and swords or whatever was to hand. Gronw the Blacksmith was not among them. Like many other Welshmen he was still a prisoner in the damp cellars of Kidwelly Castle.

'When they saw the bravery of their mother, her two eldest sons were determined to join her in battle.

'"I'm almost twelve years old," said Morgan, the eldest. "According to Welsh law I am nearly a man and I can wield a sword as well as any lad of my age."

'"I'm ten years old and I shall join you," said his brother Maelgwn.

'When she saw the fire in their eyes, Gwenllian knew that she could not refuse them. There would be many young boys in her army, for their fathers had gone away to fight with Gruffudd. It was only fair that her sons should join too.

'"Go and arm yourselves. Make haste!" she called.

'Then Gwenllian hurried to the castle nursery where Mair the nursemaid was caring for her younger sons, Anarawd, Cadell, Maredudd and Rhys. Gwenllian bade them all farewell before riding out at the head of her army.

'The local people along the route all wished her well. The plan was to sneak through the woods of Ystrad Tywi and launch a surprise attack on Maurice's castle. Along the way the peasants left their land and joined her army, bearing sickles, pitchforks and scythes.

'The courageous band came within sight of the enemy fort with their hearts beating fast at the thought of the battle that lay ahead. Yet they were not afraid, for they knew that, if they could take the castle, their countrymen would be free.

'They had reached a narrow valley between the slopes of Mynydd y Garreg and the river Gwendraeth. As Gwenllian and her men advanced slowly and cautiously, the sound of a war trumpet rang out from the mountain slopes.

'The Norman spies had learnt of Gwenllian's plan and had led her into a trap! Scores of Norman knights in full armour galloped towards Gwenllian and when she tried to turn back, the enemy came pouring down the mountainside.

'There was to be no escape, so the princess planted the Red Dragon in the flat ground at the valley bottom and shouted, "For Wales! Stand fast!"

'There was much bitter and deadly fighting that day. Gwenllian's brave men were cut down one by one and her son Morgan died defending his mother. Soon only a handful of Welshmen were left standing. In their midst were Gwenllian and her second son, Maelgwn. They were all caught and bound hand and foot. Gwenllian herself had been gravely wounded.

'"Don't you dare throw us in prison, Norman!" cried Gwenllian. "For if you do, Gruffudd and all his fellow-Welshmen, will come to our rescue. If you touch a hair of my head, my husband and my family will take their revenge!"

'A thin, cruel smile spread across Maurice's face, but he said not a word. Instead he drew his sword and chopped off Gwenllian's head in front of her son. Then he gave the sword to one of his men so he could finish off Maelgwn in the same way.'

89

Tears glistened in the eyes of Llywelyn and his men as they pondered on Gwenllian's bravery and her brutal treatment at the hands of the enemy.

'What happened to the bodies?' asked Llywelyn.

'They were buried on the field of battle,' said the storyteller. 'At the very spot where they fell. And the name of the place to this day is Gwenllian's Field.

'But although he'd killed Gwenllian and her followers, Maurice still wasn't satisfied. He wanted to teach the locals a lesson once and for all. Instead of burying Gwenllian's head, he ordered his men to take it back and nail it to the castle door as a grisly warning to any Welshman who might consider rebelling.'

*   *   *

'While the battle was raging, Gronw the Blacksmith managed to escape from Maurice's castle. Only a handful of soldiers had been left on guard, so Gronw used his great strength to smash the door of his cell and grab some clothes to disguise himself. He then fled to Ystrad Tywi Forest where he intended to hide till Gruffudd came back from the north and he could join his army.

'While he was in hiding, word reached him that Gwenllian's ghost was haunting the battlefield. Her spirit could not rest easy, because her head was still nailed to the enemy's door.

'All her people grieved for her. Not only had they lost their dear princess, but they had to witness the torment of her restless spirit. It was too much to bear.

'At last Gronw could stand it no longer. He ventured

out of hiding and returned to the castle. There he risked his life to reclaim Gwenllian's head from the castle door and take it to the battlefield for burial with her body.

'As soon as her head was buried with honour, Gwenllian's spirit rested in peace,' said Rhydderch the storyteller.

'But what about her husband and father?' asked Llywelyn. 'What did they do? Did they take revenge, as Gwenllian had promised?'

'Oh yes, my lord. When they heard of the fate of Gwenllian, they were more determined than ever to rid Wales of Maurice de Londres and his kind. The whole of Wales rose up in arms. Their campaign was called 'Gwenllian's Revenge' and no castle was safe from it.

'Driven by rage and fury Gruffudd ap Rhys and his soldiers came back from the north. With them came the huge army of Gwenllian's brother, Owain Gwynedd. They say that there were six thousand footsoldiers in that army and two thousand on horseback. It must have been an awesome sight, because rarely did the Welsh form one large army. They preferred to fight in small groups.

'The Welsh army destroyed the stronghold of Aberystwyth Castle, as well as three other Norman castles in Ceredigion, then they soundly defeated an army led by the Earl of Chester. Only five Normans escaped with their lives from that battle.

'On they went to Deheubarth and joined forces with the Brecon men to attack Cardigan. The Normans mustered a huge force to the north of the town, but they were routed by the Welshmen who yelled "Gwenllian's

Field!" as they rushed at the enemy and drove them down towards the river Teifi. Thousands of Normans lost their lives that day and the Welsh were able to drive the enemy beyond the rivers Tywi and Neath and so reclaim the lands of Deheubarth. In fact that battle was so costly to the Norman king that he decided Wales should be left alone from henceforth.

'In honour of 'Gwenllian's Revenge' her father Gruffudd ap Cynan and all the Welsh leaders from Gwynedd, Powys, Deheubarth and Glamorgan came to Ystrad Tywi to pay their respects to the memory of the brave Gwenllian and also to celebrate the defeat of their enemies.'

'I wonder if Gronw was there?' asked Llywelyn.

'Yes indeed he was, my lord. He was one of the honoured guests at the feast. The feast lasted many days. The Normans had been driven out of Wales and everyone rejoiced, though they wished Gwenllian had not had to die to achieve such a victory.'

*   *   *

If you go to Kidwelly Castle today, you will see a memorial to Gwenllian. It is her name that is honoured, not the name of the cruel Norman, Maurice de Londres. On a field at Maes Gwenllian farm, there is a stand of tall trees, which were planted by the Welsh to mark the very spot where Gwenllian fell. Nearby, hidden in a grass, is a stone circle where the princess and her followers were buried.

Oh, one more thing. Not far from the site of Gronw's forge lives another bearded giant with gingery hair.

Rugby followers will know him as Ray Gravell. Is he descended from Gronw? I wonder . . .

CILMYN
BLACKFOOT

When I was about your age, I used to enjoy playing on the banks of a little stream called Gadda. My friends and I would spend hours tickling trout or building a dam across the stream. We always had great fun as well as wet feet! Now there is a famous story about a man who got his feet wet – well, one foot at least. His name was Cilmyn Blackfoot, and this story will tell you how he came by such a strange name. Years ago every family had a coat of arms, which was the picture they painted on their shields to identify themselves. The coat of arms of the Glynllifon family in Gwynedd features a black foot, because Cilmyn was one of their ancestors. This is his story.

*   *   *

Cilmyn was an ordinary farmer, and like all farmers, he found it difficult to make ends meet. In fact, Cilmyn didn't enjoy farming. Hunting and fishing were his delight.

'If you concentrated more on ploughing and less on hunting, we could make a go of this farm,' said Gwyneth, his wife, one lunchtime.

'Yes, but it's good to have plenty of interests,' replied Cilmyn.

'Huh, it would be better if you showed some interest in your fields, instead of chasing pheasants and rabbits.'

'Yes, dear,' said Cilmyn, who knew it was no use arguing with his bossy wife.

Anyway Gwyneth was quite right. Cilmyn only cared for hunting and fishing and his dream was to have enough money to concentrate on his hobbies and give up work altogether. But how could a poor farmer hope to live on his money, especially with a wife like Gwyneth?

At that time Wales was full of witches and wise men, who were bitter enemies. The witches spent their time making mischief and the wise men spent their time trying to undo the witches' spells. Luckily every area had a wise man and so the witches didn't have it all their own way.

That evening, after quarrelling with his wife, Cilmyn didn't fancy staying in the house to listen to her nagging, so he decided to go and visit Ednyfed, the local wise man.

'I knew you'd come tonight,' said Ednyfed, as soon as Cilmyn set foot in the house. Cilmyn had learnt from experience that there was no point in asking how Ednyfed knew, so he said nothing.

'You and I are very alike, Cilmyn,' continued the wise man.

'What do you mean, Ednyfed?'

'We both have a dream. Your dream is to be a rich man and mine is to get the better of every witch in the neighbourhood. I think you could make both our dreams come true, Cilmyn. If you're brave enough, that is.'

'Could I really?' said Cilmyn, who had never thought of himself as a brave man.

'Sit down and let me explain,' said Ednyfed, waving Cilmyn towards a chair. 'As you know, there aren't many things that I can't do. I can get rid of ghosts. I can stop the fairies playing tricks on my neighbours . . .'

'And you can identify thieves and get back stolen goods,' added Cilmyn excitedly. 'Do you remember catching that farm hand who had stolen all the rent money from Hendre and hidden it in the hedge?'

'Of course I do,' scoffed Ednyfed. 'That was easy. Not half as hard as trying to keep these wicked witches under control.'

'But how can I help . . . and make my fortune?' muttered Cilmyn. His heart had sunk when he heard the word 'witches', because he was terrified of them.

'Well,' said Ednyfed, 'my plan involves a gang of witches who live on the slopes of the Eifl. They're the ones who are always causing trouble round here. Do you remember when Deio Maes Mawr's wife couldn't churn the butter?'

'Yes.'

'That was because those witches had put a spell on the

96

milk. And they were the ones who put a curse on those two horses that dropped dead during haymaking at Caerloda last year.'

'Fancy that!' said Cilmyn. 'But how I can help you deal with such wicked creatures?'

'I'll tell you,' said Ednyfed. 'The witches' curses and spells are all written down in a big book that is kept beneath a white stone in a cave at the very top of the Eifl. If I could get hold of that book, I'd know all their secrets. Then I could defeat them once and for all and make you a rich man.'

'Is that so?' said Cilmyn with a frown. 'Then why don't you go and fetch the book yourself?'

'The witches know me and as soon as they see me, they'll guess I'm after the book,' sighed the wise man. 'So the only hope is for someone like you to sneak to the top of the Eifl and snatch the book before they realise what's happening.'

By this time Cilmyn was beginning to fancy himself as a hero, especially a rich hero.

'When would be the best time to go?' he asked.

'Any time,' said Ednyfed the Wise, 'but I must warn you it won't be easy. The book is guarded by a beast, so you'll have to make sure that the creature's asleep before you make a move.'

'I'll do that,' said Cilmyn. 'I'll wait till I hear it snoring before I creep in.'

'Fair enough,' said the wise man. 'But I have one more warning.'

'Not another one?' said Cilmyn whose heart was beginning to sink again at the thought of so many dangers.

'You'll have to cross a small stream at the foot of the mountain. Be very careful not to touch the water, because the stream is enchanted and extremely dangerous. Everything that falls in the water is killed instantly. That's why you won't find a single fish in it. But the good news is that I can lend you a horse that will carry you safely over the stream in one leap. The witches and the beast are terrified of the stream and won't go near it. So what do you think? Can you do it?'

'Yes, I'm game,' said Cilmyn after a second's pause.

'Good for you,' said Ednyfed. 'You'll do us all a favour and I'll make sure that you're the richest man in the area.'

Cilmyn left Ednyfed's house and went home to face Gwyneth's sharp tongue, but for once he didn't care. In his own mind he was already a rich man. Never again would he have to bother about sowing and reaping. He could spend his time fishing for salmon along the banks of the Llyfni . . .

* * *

The next morning Cilmyn got up with the lark and told Gwyneth he was off to the market in Pwllheli.

'Pwllheli? What on earth for?' said Gwyneth. 'Caernarfon is so much nearer.'

'I'm thinking of buying a new scythe for the haymaking,' he replied. 'There's a better choice in Pwllheli. And they're cheaper.'

'At last! You're thinking about work instead of lazing around on that river!'

Little did Gwyneth know that her husband was about

to set off for the slopes of the Eifl to steal the magic book for Ednyfed the Wise. So when she saw him wolf down two bowlfuls of porridge for breakfast instead of his usual one, and head in the direction of Pwllheli, she thought nothing of it.

Einion stopped at the wise man's house to borrow the horse, then went on his way, past the old church of Clynnog and on to Llanaelhaearn. As soon as he reached the slopes of the Eifl, he knew he had to be very, very careful indeed.

First of all he had to cross the deadly stream. The stream wasn't difficult to spot. It crept down the slopes like a giant snake, leaving a trail of black grass on its poisoned banks. Cilmyn urged the horse on and with one graceful leap it cleared the stream.

Now he had to look out for the witches. He decided it was safer to continue on foot and so he tied the horse to a tree. There it would wait till he returned with the magic book.

He hadn't gone far when he heard wild laughter from behind a hedge and the sound of harsh, gloating voices chanting a poem.

'Hywel the Red from the farm on the hill –
Wander and wander for ever he will.
Each step that he takes will lead to a stile,
All of the stiles will break him a bone
Not the biggest of bones, nor the smallest of bones,
But the bone of his neck every time.'

The witches were cursing Cilmyn's neighbour. There wasn't a second to lose. The magic book must be taken to Ednyfed before the witches could harm Hywel!

Cilmyn sneaked past the devilish band and headed for the slopes of the Eifl. He knew he'd be fairly safe till he reached the cave and had to tackle the beast that was guarding the book.

He struggled on and on up the slopes and by the time he reached the highest peak, he was beginning to get scared. Above him was the mouth of the enormous cave where the book was kept. What if the beast saw him? That would be the end of him. Cilmyn squatted behind a rock and listened hard. At first the only sound he could hear was the thumping of his own heart. It was so loud he was afraid it would alert the beast, but then the sound of deep, heavy breathing and noisy snores reached his ears. The guardian of the book was fast asleep.

Cilmyn crept into the cave and waited for his eyes to grow accustomed to the dark. Fear gnawed at his stomach when he smelled a terrible smell. Whatever the beast was, it stank like a polecat. When he spotted the creature, he felt worse still and nearly screamed in terror. The beast was huge – at least twice as tall as the tallest man he'd ever seen – and it was covered in long reddish-brown hair from its head to its toes. But worst of all were the long teeth that glistened through the fur. The beast had been gnawing on the leg of a cow and Cilmyn knew he'd make short work of any poor farmer who tried to steal the magic book.

But where was the book? Where was the white stone? When Cilmyn caught sight of it, he nearly gave up and ran away. The white stone was lying beneath the beast's claw.

Cilmyn gathered his courage, inched forward, held

his breath and carefully lifted the claw. The beast stirred but did not wake up. Next Cilmyn shifted the stone, and although it was an enormous stone, he did so without any noise at all. Now he could see the magic book shining in the hole beneath. Its covers were made of gold and studded with pearls and precious stones.

But this was not the time to admire the book. He bent down, snatched it up and turned to make his escape. At once a voice boomed.

'What do you think you're doing?'

The hairs stood up on the back of Cilmyn's neck. The beast had woken up and rushed to block the cave mouth.

'I'm just going to give the book to my friend Ednyfed over there,' said Cilmyn, nodding at a spot behind the beast's shoulder.

The beast turned round to see who was there and at once Cilmyn shot past him with the book beneath his arm. He thundered down the slopes of the Eifl with the beast hard on his heels and yelling at the top of his voice.

'Witches! Witches! Stop him! He's stolen the magic book!'

'Shut your mouth!' said Cilmyn and stopped dead at the very edge of a steep drop. The beast was going too fast to stop. It hurtled past and fell headlong down the mountainside.

'Next I've got to pass those witches and find my horse!' panted Cilmyn. At that moment he saw, a huge group of witches dressed in black with pointed hats coming towards him. To his dismay one of them was leading the horse.

'Cilmyn, you give me the book and you can ride home safely on your horse,' she called.

No chance, thought Cilmyn. My only hope is to run for my life towards the river and pray that the witches don't catch me.

And so he ran for his life with the witches in hot pursuit. The magic book weighed him down and he could hear their curses ringing in his ears. Still he kept going. Even when their yellow nails scraped his back, he ran on.

'What are you going to do now, Cilmyn?' screeched a witch. 'We're nearing the stream. You have no horse and if you fall in the water, you'll die.'

'So I will,' muttered Cilmyn under his breath. 'But what else can I do?'

On he ran as he had never run before. He launched himself through the air and aimed for the safety of the far bank. His right foot landed on solid ground but, because of the weight of the magic book, his left leg slipped into the water up to the knee. He pulled it out at once, but the poisoned water had already done its work and the leg had begun to wither away.

'Curse you, Cilmyn!' the witches screeched like wild cats.

'You can shout as much as you like,' Cilmyn retorted, 'but when Ednyfed the Wise gets hold of this book, that'll be the end of your cursing and your evil spells.' And waving the book happily, he began to limp back home.

* * *

You can just imagine the welcome that awaited Cilmyn at Ednyfed's house. In no time the wise man had used the magic book to cancel out all the witches' spells and tricks. He also honoured his promise to make Cilmyn a rich man by giving him the golden jewelled covers of the magic book. Cilmyn was now so rich he built a mansion for himself and Gwyneth. This was the mansion of Glynllifon and although Gwyneth now lived in great comfort, she still grumbled that her husband spent too much time on the river bank!

But I expect you want to know what happened to Cilmyn's leg. Well, despite all the information he gleaned from the magic book, Ednyfed could not cure his friend's leg. Cilmyn was lame for the rest of his life. His leg had turned black when it slipped into the water, and black it remained. That is why he was nicknamed Cilmyn Blackfoot and that is why there is a black leg on the Glynllifon coat of arms.

SAINT BEUNO AND
THE HOLY WELL

Long ago people would make an effort to visit holy places. These people were known as pilgrims. Often the pilgrims would travel as far as Jerusalem or Rome, and their journey was long and hard. Sometimes it was dangerous too and many lost their lives along the way. At a time when there were no aeroplanes, pilgrims had to travel for many weeks over land and sea, over high mountains and arid deserts.

In Wales pilgrims used to flock to two places. These were . . . the Millennium Stadium and Stradey Park! No, of course not. The two places were St Davids in Pembrokeshire, the birthplace of our patron saint, and Bardsey Island in the north, where they say that twenty thousand saints lie buried.

Every year hundreds of pilgrims would flock to these two places to see the wonders displayed there. If you lived seven centuries ago, you would probably spend your holiday walking to St Davids to see the bones of the saint. To reach both places, you would follow the Pilgrims' Way, stopping here and there to visit sites of interest and importance.

If you were heading for Bardsey Island, you would have to visit the village of Clynnog, or Clynnog Fawr in Arfon as it was once called. Clynnog is important because of its connection with Saint Beuno. Before Beuno went to Clynnog, no one lived there. It was a place of trees and wild moorland. Beuno himself was a remarkable man and this is his story.

*   *   *

Beuno was the son of a prince of Glamorgan and, like many of our early saints, he himself could have been a rich prince. But at the time there was bitter fighting between the Welsh and the English, which made him very unhappy. Beuno wanted everyone to live in peace and so, once he had completed his education, he decided to leave the comforts of the court and become a poor monk.

For a short while he lived in Berriew near the English border, but when the English launched an attack he was forced to flee north to Flintshire. He settled in a place which is now called Holywell. It is because of Beuno that the town is known by that name.

A young woman called Winifred lived nearby. She, like Beuno, tried to persuade people to lead better lives.

Not only were the two of them good friends who shared the same interests, but they were also related. Beuno was Winifred's uncle.

One hot day, Beuno was busy digging in the garden of the monastery, when he heard a shout.

'What was that?' he asked his friend, Twrog.

'I'm not sure,' Twrog replied, 'but I think someone's calling your name.'

The noise came closer.

'Beuno! Beuno! Come at once! Something terrible has happened!'

Now Beuno recognised the voice. It belonged to Gwenan, one of the girls who helped Winifred with her good work. He rushed to meet her.

'What is it, Gwenan?' he asked.

'Winifred has been killed!'

'What?'

'It's true!' sobbed Gwenan. 'Winifred went to the camp of Caradog the chieftain to try and make him mend his ways, but Caradog and his men attacked her and cut her head off. Oh Beuno, what shall we do?'

Beuno wasted no time. He went directly to the camp. Caradog and his men were standing around looking worried and ashamed. They knew that they had done wrong. Beuno did not say a word to them. Instead he hurried to the body of Winifred which was lying on the ground with her head some distance away. Carefully Beuno picked up the head, replaced it on Winifred's shoulders and held it tight. He closed his eyes and prayed for his niece to be restored to life.

To everyone's joy Beuno's prayers were answered and Winifred rose to her feet. That was Beuno's first miracle.

The second occurred soon after.

'Look!' cried Twrog. 'A spring of water has appeared on the very spot where Winifred's head lay.'

'Yes,' said Beuno. 'And that spring is a healing spring, which will cure many diseases.'

The spring can still be seen. A small town grew around it, a town called Holywell. And it is still a healing spring. If you go there, you will see crutches lying on the ground. They were left by lame people who found they could walk after bathing in the water of Winifred's Well.

*   *   *

Neither Winifred nor Beuno stayed long in Holywell. Shortly after Winifred had been restored to life, Caradog and his family were afflicted by a terrible plague as a warning to others not to follow in their footsteps. The only cure was to drink the water of Winifred's Well.

When the people heard of all that had happened, they flocked to see the good man who had performed such miracles. Beuno could get no peace and so he moved to Gwynedd.

Now, if you or I wanted to move, we'd buy a new house. But there was no way a poor monk such as Beuno could buy a house. So he went instead to Cadwallon, prince of Gwynedd, to ask for a plot of land.

'Beuno, I'm so pleased to meet you,' said the prince, when Beuno arrived at his court in Aberffraw. 'What do you want of me?'

'I'd like a quiet place where I can build a monastery,' replied Beuno.

'I have just the place for you,' replied the prince. 'It's

a small place called Gwredog on the banks of the Gwyrfai river in a fine wooded valley.'

'It sounds perfect,' said Beuno. 'Thank you.'

'Think nothing of it,' said Cadwallon. 'Gwredog is yours.'

Off went Beuno to the promised land with Twrog beside him.

When they reached Gwredog, Beuno and his friends began to build a monastery. But, each morning, as soon as they started work, a young mother appeared with a baby in her arms. The moment the men rolled up their sleeves, the baby started crying at the top of his voice.

This went on for a whole week. By the end of the week Beuno and his companions had had enough. This crying was enough to try the patience of a saint!

'What is the matter with your baby?' Beuno asked the mother. 'He's making our work impossible. All this crying and bawling has given me a headache.'

'You'd be crying and bawling too, if someone had stolen your land,' said the young woman.

'But this is my land,' said Beuno. 'It was given to me by Cadwallon.'

'Huh! It wasn't Cadwallon's land to give,' she snapped.

'Why not?' asked the saint.

The young woman explained that the land belonged to her baby's father. Cadwallon had killed him and stolen the land that should have come to the baby. That was why he was crying.

Well, Beuno was furious! He marched all the way to Aberffraw where he told the prince what he thought of thieving cheats, then marched away again.

He was still muttering angrily to himself, when he heard the sound of hoofbeats.

'Beuno! Beuno! Wait!' cried a voice.

A young man rode up and leapt from his horse.

'My name is Gwyddaint,' he said. 'I am the prince's cousin and I am very ashamed of the way he has behaved. I have some land you can have and it is not stolen land.'

'Thank you, Gwyddaint,' said Beuno. 'Where is this land?'

'It's at Clynnog on the coast.'

'Excellent! The monks will be able to fish as well as till the soil. Bless you, Gwyddaint.

The two shook hands and, to mark the spot, the saint drew a cross on a nearby stone using only his thumb.

That is how Beuno came to live in Clynnog. The stone with the mark of the cross was later moved to the church, where it can still be seen. Gwredog, on the other hand, played its part in the life of another saint. It grew into a small settlement, close to the present-day village of Waunfawr, and it was from there, so they say, that Patrick, the patron saint of Ireland, was captured by pirates. But that is another story!

*   *   *

Soon there was a monastery, or clas as it was called, in Clynnog. All the monks worked hard, but no one worked harder than Beuno. He built a special fish trap called a 'cored' on the beach, and that can still be seen to this day.

The monks bred many different animals, each with a

special mark on its back. That mark was called 'Beuno's Mark' and it proved that the animals belonged to the saint. Many centuries after the death of the saint, they say that several animals born in the Clynnog area still had Beuno's mark on their backs. When these animals were sold, the money was put in a wooden chest that had belonged to the saint. That chest is still in the church.

Beuno often used to go over to Anglesey to preach. To get there he walked across a causeway, which was known as Sarn Beuno. On his way across one day a valuable book fell from his hand and dropped into the sea. Before it sank without trace, a curlew swooped, picked it up in its beak and dropped it at the saint's feet. To show his appreciation, the saint said:

'Your nest will be safe from this very day
And no hunter will find you an easy prey.'

Since then a curlew's nest has been difficult to find. The causeway itself has sunk beneath the waves, though it is sometimes marked on old maps.

* * *

Every night after supper, Beuno used to leave the monastery and look for a quiet place in which to pray. He wanted no one near him.

But one night a monk followed him. He watched Beuno head for the slopes of the Eifl and fall to his knees in a sheltered spot.

The monk knew he had broken the rules. He felt rather uneasy, but he had little chance to repent, for a

pack of wolves fell on him there and then and tore him to bits.

Beuno heard the terrible screams and snarls from the woods. With no thought for his own safety he rushed to see what was happening. It was already too late. The wolves fled when they heard him approach and left the remains of the monk scattered across the forest floor.

Beuno was left with the unpleasant task of gathering the pieces in order to try and restore the life of the monk. Soon he had found every piece apart from the forehead, which was nowhere to be seen. As he looked around him, Beuno noticed the iron ferrule that protected the tip of his walking stick. The ferrule was just the right size, so he pulled it off and fitted it into the hole in the monk's forehead.

Once the monk was restored to life he was rechristened Aelhaearn, which means Iron Brow. Later he built a church on the spot where he was attacked by the wolves. A village sprang up around the church and to this day it is known as Llanaelhaearn.

*   *   *

For many years life was quiet and serene in the monastery at Clynnog. The monks saw to the running of the monastery and for those who had chosen this way of life, there was no better place to live.

For Beuno it was all he had ever wanted. The local people listened to his every word, so he no longer needed to perform miracles. Instead he could concentrate on building churches in North Wales.

When he was old and weak, he decided to go on one

last journey to see his friends. After he had visited them all, he died peacefully in Beddgelert.

But all was not peaceful after his death. The good people of Beddgelert wanted to bury him in their village. The people of Bardsey objected! They wanted him to be the twenty thousand and first saint to lie on their island. The monks of Clynnog on the other hand wanted their founder to rest in peace in his very own church.

All the monks of Clynnog went to Beddgelert to demand the body of Beuno. They picked up the coffin and started on their homeward journey. The people of Beddgelert and the people of Bardsey insisted on accompanying them and they were all still arguing when night fell.

They spent the night at a place called Ynys yr Arch or Coffin Island and, when they woke up in the morning, to their astonishment they discovered three coffins instead of one. Poor old Beuno had had to perform another miracle to make sure that no one was disappointed!

The people of Clynnog still insist that their village is Beuno's true resting-place. Attached to the village church is a small chapel and they say that that is where the remains of the saint lie. The chapel is called the Chapel of the Grave.

*   *   *

There is one other place in Clynnog which is named after Beuno, and that is Beuno's Well. The pilgrims of old used to sip the water and pray in the church for a safe crossing to Bardsey.

Until fairly recently many believed that the water

could cure diseases and, as in the case of Winifred's Well, the banks would be littered with the crutches and sticks of those who had been healed.

The Age of the Pilgrim has now long gone, but the church at Clynnog is still well worth a visit. As well as all the objects associated with Beuno, you will see the tongs that were used to remove mad dogs from the church.

τbε Gbosτly Guiɒε

When people go to England, we sometimes say that they've 'crossed Offa's Dyke'. Offa was an English king who lived many centuries ago. At the time the Welsh were a thorn in his side, because they used to raid the lands of his people and steal their animals. To keep the Welsh out, Offa built a dyke, or a great wall, which follows the Welsh-English border from north to south. That is why we talk of crossing Offa's Dyke.

Today there is a public footpath that runs the whole length of the dyke for more than a hundred and eighty miles from the Bristol Channel in the south to Liverpool Bay in the north. It isn't an easy walk, because the dyke travels up hill and down dale and crosses lonely mountainous regions, especially in the Black Mountains in the south. It's not a good place in which to get lost.

*   *   *

Over the centuries many Welsh people settled on the English side of Offa's Dyke, especially in the Black Mountains. Amongst them were the ancestors of Richard Shenkin who had settled in Pen y Lan on Mynydd Merddin. Despite its name Mynydd Merddin is in England and, though they lived in England, Richard and his family still kept in close contact with their friends in Wales.

At dinner time on a cold windy day in January, Richard said to his wife, 'Mali, I'm going over to see Hywel of Nant y Carnau.'

'You're not!' she replied. 'Why do you want to go so far in this awful weather? It's not looking good and there's mist over the dyke. Eat up your mash, for goodness sake, and stay right there.'

'There's no need to fuss, Mali my dear,' replied Richard. 'Hywel has a book on the history of Llanthony Priory that he's offered to sell me.'

'You and your history! Wait till next Saturday. The weather could be better by then.'

'No, Mali. If I don't go today someone else will have got his hands on the book and I'll have missed my chance. Don't you worry. I'll be back tonight and I'll have the horn lantern with me to light my way. Anyway I'm going over to the Nant and that's that.'

Without more ado Richard put on a warm coat, threw an old sack over his shoulders to keep out the cold and set off boldly in the direction of Offa's Dyke and Wales.

He walked down his fields towards the Monnow river and crossed at Clydach bridge, then began to climb the gentle slope towards Pen y Rhiwiau. Soon the land rose steeply towards Rhiw Arw Ridge and the Welsh border. Above him the remains of the dyke that Offa had built so many centuries ago were cloaked in thick mist. This didn't worry Richard, because he knew the area like the back of his hand.

The mist settled around him like damp cotton wool, but Richard found the path without any trouble and soon he was scrambling over the dyke and the deep ditch beyond. Now the path led him down towards Ty Isaf and the ruins of the beautiful priory of Llanthony. He was soaked to the skin, but that didn't bother him either. His mind was on the fine book that was waiting for him at Nant y Carnau.

*   *   *

'Sit yourself down by the fire, Richard man. I'm sure you're frozen to the bone after crossing the mountain in this weather,' said Hywel Wyn when he opened his door.

'Thank you, Hywel. The last hour of the journey was rather cold,' said Richard, removing the wet sack and taking off his coat.

In no time Alis, Hywel's wife, had served him a bowl of stew from the cooking pot that simmered on the peat fire.

Though the stew was good, the conversation was even better as the two men swapped stories about the history and traditions of the region.

'I don't want to disturb you,' said Alis after they'd

talked for a while. 'But it's getting dark. Would you like to stay the night, Richard?'

'Oh goodness me! I'd forgotten the time,' replied Richard. 'No, thank you, Alis. I can't stay. I've got to go home tonight. I promised Mali I'd be home and she'll be worried stiff if I don't keep my word.'

Richard and Hywel had already agreed a price, so the book was now Richard's. He wrapped it carefully and slid it into the inside pocket of his coat to keep it dry. He lit the candle in the horn lantern and called, 'Good night! Thank you again for the book!' as he set off happily on the long journey to Pen y Lan.

The wind had risen and the candle was flickering long before he reached Ty Isaf. To make matters worse, the mist was lower and thicker than ever. Still Richard walked on. He must get back at all costs before Mali started worrying. As he began climbing towards the ridge, the wind grew wilder and wilder. One strong gust blew out his candle. He couldn't possibly relight it in such stormy weather, so there was nothing for it but to struggle on through the dark night.

He had only taken a few steps, when he tripped and went rolling down the steep hill. His lantern was smashed and the breath knocked out of him, but at least he was still in one piece. He got up slowly. Where was he? The fall had confused him. The path was above him, but where? To his left or to his right? He had no idea. With a thumping heart Richard realised he was lost in the cold, the mist and the darkness.

He was ready to sink to the ground in despair, when he saw a faint light bobbing in the mist. Someone was walking above him on the hill. Richard made sure the book was safe in his pocket, then scrambled up towards the light as best he could.

Soon he found himself on the path where a tall man of around his own age was waiting for him. The man wore dark old-fashioned clothes and by the light of the lantern that he held in his hand, Richard could see an ugly scar on his forehead. Despite the scar his face was kindly.

'Thank you, good friend,' panted Richard. 'I thought I'd have to spend the night on the mountain in this storm. My name is Richard Shenkin.'

The stranger said not a word, but turned on his heel and walked off up the hill. He must be in a hurry to get home, thought Richard.

Richard tried to catch him up, so they could exchange a few words, but however fast he walked, the stranger walked faster. Still he was heading towards Offa's Dyke and that was all that mattered.

After many minutes of hard walking, Richard felt the ground flatten beneath his feet and knew he was standing on the ridge. Without pausing for breath the stranger pressed on with the wind in his face and Richard rushed after him in case he was stranded in the mist.

As they were running down the slopes of Rhiw Arw, Richard tried to strike up a conversation once more.

'Sir! I live on this side of the dyke, on Mynydd Merddin, but I don't think I know you. Will you tell me your name?'

The stranger did not reply. He merely raced farther ahead till his lantern was just a dot in the darkness.

'Wait for me!' yelled Richard, running as fast as he could and hoping against hope that he wouldn't trip again.

And then the mist lifted. Richard saw lights below him and although it was still dark, he knew where he was. He only had to cross the river Monnow and he would be safely home.

He turned round to thank the stranger with the lantern, but to his surprise there was no sign of him anywhere.

'I wonder where he went?' murmured Richard to himself. 'He could have gone towards the Olchon Valley, I suppose, but why can't I see his light? I'm so glad I met him, whoever he was. I should be home safe and sound within half an hour.'

*   *   *

Mali was very pleased to welcome her husband home that night, although she did grumble in the days and weeks that followed that he was spending too much time with his nose in his book instead of working!

Whenever he read his book, Richard would remember his narrow escape on the mountainside. If it hadn't been for the stranger and his lantern, he could so easily have frozen to death. He asked his neighbours if they knew who the man might be, but no one could tell him. He asked around the Olchon Valley, in case the stranger had headed in that direction, but no one knew him there either.

He only found the answer to the mystery the following May when he returned to see his friend Hywel at Nant y Carnau.

'Describe this man to me,' said Hywel.

'He was a tall man, about my age, dressed in dark

clothes that looked rather old-fashioned,' said Richard.

'What about the scar on his face?'

'It was an ugly scar, as I remember, though the man's face was kindly. But I didn't have time to study him closely. He rushed off ahead of me as if the devil were after him and once the mist had cleared, he disappeared.'

'Sit down, Richard,' said Hywel solemnly.

'Why? What's wrong?'

'Do you know who guided you over the mountain?'

'No.'

'Ednyfed ap Caradog.'

'But that's impossible!' gasped Richard. 'He died years ago.'

'Maybe,' said Hywel, 'but, if you remember, he was kicked by a horse as a child and had a scar on his forehead. Ednyfed died on the mountain one cold night when he was trying to cross towards the Olchon Valley.'

Richard felt an icy tingle down his spine as he waited for Hywel's next words.

'Where exactly did the guide disappear?'

'On Rhiw Arw,' whispered Richard.

'And that's exactly where they found the body of poor Ednyfed,' said Hywel. 'Richard Shenkin, you were guided through the mist by the ghost of a man who died half a century ago!'

The Two Halves of the Ring

Long ago every prince of Wales had a storyteller in his court, and also a poet, or a bard. The bard would retell stories of ancient heroes, entertain his audience with tales and compose all sorts of poems. One of the most famous of these bards was Meilir. He was the bard at the court of Aberffraw nearly nine hundred years ago. Prince Gruffudd ap Cynan thought highly of him and gave him land and a fine house at Trefeilir on Anglesey.

After the death of Meilir, his son, Gwalchmai ap Meilir became the court poet. He so impressed the prince that he too was given money and land at Trewalchmai. The village of Gwalchmai on Anglesey still bears his name.

And if that was not enough, Gwalchmai too had a famous son. His name was Einion – or to give him his full name, Einion ap Gwalchmai – and yes, he too was a famous poet. He lived in his grandfather's home at Trefeilir and that is where our story begins.

* * *

Einion was a very rich man who had inherited land from both his father and grandfather. He had also married the daughter of one of the most important men in Gwynedd. Her name was Angharad and her father was Ednyfed Fychan, the chief steward of Gwynedd. The chief steward was as important as a prime minister.

One day Einion was out deer hunting in the woods near his home. He needed a supply of venison for a banquet that was to be held that night in honour of his father-in-law's birthday. Einion had invited his father-in-law to Trefeilir to celebrate the occasion.

Now, I don't suppose you've ever hunted deer. The deer is a very timid animal that is easily frightened. The hunter has to creep up on it without being seen, which takes time and patience. Einion certainly had to be patient that day. He had to venture deep into the woods to find his prey. As soon as he saw movement, he crouched down, raised his bow and took aim. He was about to loose the deadly arrow, when to his shock and amazement a young woman stepped out of the trees. She was the most beautiful girl Einion had ever seen.

'Who are you?' he asked.

'Never you mind,' was the answer.

'But I nearly killed you!' protested Einion. 'You have no right to be here.'

'No right? Is that so?' The young woman gazed into

Einion's eyes till he felt himself go weak at the knees.

Her deep blue eyes were enchanting – so enchanting that Einion had to bow his head to hide his blushes. As he did so, he saw something that made him gasp out loud.

'But . . .'

'But what?' she whispered in a voice as sweet as honey.

'Your feet! They're hoofs!' cried Einion. The creature before him was not a young woman. It was an evil sprite.

'What if they are?' sneered the sprite. 'You are now forever in my power and must do exactly as I say.'

'That's what you think,' retorted Einion. 'I'm going home to my wife this very minute.'

'Off you go then,' the sprite said calmly.

To Einion's dismay he found he could not move a muscle. He had been bewitched.

'As you see, Einion ap Gwalchmai,' said the sprite, 'you can't move unless I say so. Whether you like it or not, you are coming with me.'

'So it seems!' said poor Einion. 'But please will you grant me one wish? Let me go home to say goodbye to Angharad and my little son.'

'All right, you sentimental fool,' the sprite replied with a cruel smile. 'But remember this. I shall not leave your side. You'll be able to see me, but no one else will, so there's no hope of escape.'

A heartbroken Einion walked back to his house and went at once in search of Angharad.

'My dear Angharad,' he said, 'I've just received an urgent message from the prince himself. He wants me to go to the Lands of the North.' He did not want to distress his wife by telling her the truth.

'But why, Einion?' she cried.

'It's a secret. I'm not allowed to tell anyone, not even you,' said Einion. As he spoke, he could see the sprite smirking at him, though Angharad could see nothing.

'When are you going?'

'This very minute. I'm afraid I must say goodbye, Angharad.'

'But shouldn't you be taking some warm clothes?' asked his wife in a panic.

'The prince will see to that.'

'This can't be right. When will you be back?'

'I don't know,' murmured Einion. He glanced at the hoofed sprite, but the sprite merely sneered.

By this time Angharad was weeping bitterly. She took off her wedding ring and ordered her servant to split it in two.

'You take one half and I'll keep the other,' she said to Einion. 'As soon as you return, we shall make the ring whole again, but while you're away, we shall each have a half as a keepsake to remind us of each other.'

On hearing this, the sprite spat on the floor and signalled to Einion that they must leave at once.

'I must go, Angharad,' said Einion and hurried away leaving the whole household in tears. What else could he do?

*   *   *

The sprite's spell was so strong that Einion lost all sense of time and place. Days, weeks and years passed in a haze. He understood little of what was happening, but he knew that the sprite was always at his side.

Throughout this time he was aware of the half-ring in

his pocket and one day he said to himself, 'If I can put this in my eye, maybe I'll see Angharad again. I'd do anything to see my wife and son.'

He had the ring in his hand and was bracing himself for the pain, when a handsome knight came riding towards him on a tall white horse. The knight was dressed in white from top to toe.

'My dear friend, what on earth are you doing with that ring?' cried the knight. 'Be careful or you'll injure your eye.'

'I'm trying to see my wife, Angharad,' said poor Einion, and he poured out the whole sad story to the knight.

'If what you say is true,' said the White Knight, 'put that ring back in your pocket and climb up behind me.'

Einion did so immediately.

'Now take this magic wand in your hand,' said the knight. 'Make a wish and you shall see what you most desire.'

As he spoke, who should appear but the sprite. For the first time Einion saw the creature in all its ugliness. This was no beautiful young woman. It was a loathsome and terrifying beast with horns growing out of its forehead and a clump of writhing, hissing snakes for hair. Its teeth were the teeth of a shark and its tail was longer and thinner than a snake. Einion cried out in terror at the sight of it.

The horse galloped off with the sprite pounding after it. A sharp claw scratched Einion's back, but the knight threw his cloak over him to protect him.

Einion felt the scratch of a claw once more and then – in the blink of an eye – the sprite had gone. The knight and his cloak had vanished too and Einion found himself standing in the grounds of his old home. As he stumbled towards the house, no one recognised the bearded, scruffy wild man of the woods with a strange white stick in his hand.

*   *   *

While Einion was away on his terrible adventure, much had happened to Angharad. At first she had struggled on from day to day, hoping against hope that she would have news of her husband. To her surprise her father knew nothing of Einion's whereabouts, even though he was chief steward to the king. Einion must be on a very secret mission indeed, his wife thought.

Gradually, as the weeks became months and the months became years without a word from Einion, Angharad began to fear that her husband had met with an accident. Her worst fears were confirmed when one day a strange nobleman came to Trefeilir and presented her with this letter.

The Court of Aberffraw

Dear Angharad,

I fear I have sad news. Nine years ago I sent Einion on a secret mission to the Lands of the North. The journey should only have taken him three months and though there was no news of him, I could not bring myself to believe that all was not well.

Lately I sent a man in search of him and I have just learnt, to my great dismay, that poor Einion was killed by my enemies nine years ago.

I am sorry to be the bearer of such tragic news.

LLYWELYN AP IORWERTH –
PRINCE OF GWYNEDD

The message bore the prince's seal and the messenger himself looked so noble that Angharad accepted it without question. After all these years she was not surprised to learn of her husband's death.

And yet, as we know, Einion was not dead. So why had the prince written such a letter? The prince had done no such thing. The message was a fake and the nobleman was the sprite himself who had assumed a disguise in order to deceive Angharad.

'I'm truly sorry to bring you such sad news,' said the treacherous creature. 'As it happens I am the man who was sent in search of Einion. I can assure you he died very bravely.'

The lying sprite found an excuse to stay in Trefeilir that night and Angharad enjoyed his company so much, she persuaded him to stay for a week. That was exactly what the sprite had hoped. Soon he had bewitched Angharad, just as he had bewitched her husband. This time he kept his cloven feet well hidden and within a few days Angharad, believing she was now a widow, had accepted his proposal of marriage. She also believed the sprite when he told her he owned a fine mansion where his many servants brought him food on golden dishes.

They set the date for the wedding and began to make preparations. A dress of rich silk was made for Angharad. Food and drink were brought in from all corners of the world. The best musicians were hired to entertain the guests at Trefeilir. This was going be the grandest wedding ever seen outside the court of Aberffraw.

Everything was ready for the big day, when the sprite

noticed a beautiful harp in Angharad's room. He went to play it, but the harp stayed silent. The sprite snarled under his breath and summoned the musicians to him. They too failed to play the harp.

'You're wasting your time,' Angharad called to them. 'My husband Einion was the only one who understood that harp. It won't play for anyone else.'

'Oh, forget Einion!' snapped the sprite. 'After lunch we'll be heading for the church and then I'll be your husband.'

Before Angharad could reply, there was a knock at the door and in came a servant, followed by a bearded stranger.

'This man has come to ask for work, my lady,' said the servant.

Angharad looked closely at the man. His clothes were filthy and in tatters and his hair and beard hung in straggly rats' tails. He looked like a poor tramp who'd been on the road for many a long year. But Angharad was a kind woman, so she told him to go to the cook and ask if he could help with the preparations for lunch and then for the wedding feast.

'Thank you, lady,' the stranger replied in a weak voice.

In his hand was a mysterious, white stick. The stranger was indeed Einion, but he had changed so much that Angharad did not recognise him. He did not tell her who he was, but went to the kitchen, where he worked hard to prepare the many dishes.

When lunch was ready, Einion helped to carry the food to the table. In the corner of the room the musicians were still trying to coax a note from the harp. Without a word Einion took the harp in his arms, tuned it and played one of his favourite melodies. As the notes floated across the room, everyone was astonished and no one more so than Angharad. She looked closely at the stranger.

'Who are you?' she asked.

'Einion, your husband,' he replied.

Silence fell on the room. How could this stranger be Einion? How can he be my husband, thought Angharad. My husband has been dead for nine years.

'Look, Angharad,' said Einion, pulling the half-ring from his pocket. 'This is my half, remember? Where is yours?'

'Here!' she said, plucking her half-ring from her own pocket.

The two halves fitted perfectly.

'But the Prince sent me a letter to say you were dead!' said Angharad in a trembling voice.

'Are you sure?' asked Einion. 'Who brought it? Was it that man?' He nodded towards the sprite.

'Yes.'

Einion placed his white stick in Angharad's hand.

'Now point this at him and take another look,' he said.

Angharad did so and with a scream she fell in a faint. She too had seen the sprite in all his ugliness.

* * *

When Angharad came round, the room was empty apart from herself and Einion.

'Where is everyone?' she cried.

'They've gone,' he replied.

'And where is that terrible creature?'

'He didn't hang around once you'd had a good look at him,' said Einion. 'When I touched him with this magic wand, he disappeared in a ball of fire. All that is left is a rotten smell!'

From that moment on Einion and Angharad put all their bad memories behind them and lived happily together for the rest of their lives.

The Adventures of Prince Maelgwn

Names are strange things, aren't they? Imagine what would happen if you had no name. No one could call you when food was ready, the postman wouldn't bring you birthday cards – and your teacher couldn't give you a row! Yes, names are strange things, but they're also important and many have stories associated with them. For instance, if there is a Non in your class, she is named after Non, the mother of St David. Owain is the name of many Welsh heroes including the most important of all, Owain Glyndwr. Myrddin, is Welsh for Merlin, who was King Arthur's wizard. So anyone called Myrddin should be a wizard at tricks!

Maelgwn is an unusual name. Do you know a boy called Maelgwn? If you do, you can tell him that he's named after one of the old princes of Gwynedd. Many stories are told about Maelgwn. These are some of them.

*   *   *

Maelgwn was born about one thousand five hundred years ago, at a time when many strange things were happening in Gwynedd and other parts of Wales. His father, Cadwallon, was prince of Gwynedd. Even as a boy Maelgwn was tall and fearless. Because he was so tall, he was given the nickname Maelgwn Hir, or Long Maelgwn.

He was a very clever boy and was sent to a famous school run by Saint Illtyd in the Vale of Glamorgan. The school was part of the monastery founded by Saint Illtyd. A town grew around it and that town is known today as Llanilltyd Fawr, or Llantwit Major. In Maelgwn's time there was no town. There was only a monastery and Maelgwn couldn't wait to get away from there. Not because he was a cry-baby. Far from it! The truth was that he had no interest in reading and writing Latin. All he wanted to do was fight and hunt. Maelgwn longed to be back in Gwynedd hunting dragons and wolves in the mountains and fighting any enemy that threatened his land. But as with all schoolboys in every age, Maelgwn had to stay at his desk untill he'd finished all his exams.

Even after leaving school, Maelgwn still had lessons to learn. He had to learn how to be a prince so he could follow in his father's footsteps. That didn't stop him having fun and many adventures. At that time dragons and huge vipers, which were half-dragon and half-snake, used to terrorise the land. Maelgwn had many close shaves while hunting them. He was a hot-headed boy, who didn't know the meaning of fear. Maybe that was why he always escaped with his life!

*　　*　　*

One day, when Maelgwn was a young man, his father Cadwallon called him.

'Maelgwn, it's time you found a wife,' he said.

'What for?' groaned Maelgwn. 'I'm far too busy for marriage and all that nonsense!'

'Nonsense, indeed!' boomed the king. 'A prince must have a wife and I've found just the girl for you.'

'What? Who is she?'

'Her name is Nest and she is the most beautiful girl in Wales.'

As soon as he heard Nest's name – and before he'd even seen her – a great change came over Maelgwn. Instead of riding over the hills to fight wild beasts, he started hanging around the court with a dreamy look in his eyes. The poor boy was in love! Luckily for Maelgwn Nest felt just the same, so they were soon married.

Nest loved swimming and although she was now a princess, she got up at the crack of dawn each morning, left the court at Deganwy and set off for the beach. Summer or winter, whatever the weather, Nest would go swimming.

One morning the wind was blowing hard and the waves rushing towards the beach like foamy white horses. That didn't stop Nest from enjoying her usual morning dip, but as soon as she stepped out of the water, she realised something was wrong. The waves had snatched the wedding ring from her finger.

'What shall I do now?' whimpered Nest to herself. 'That ring belonged to the princesses of Gwynedd. It was very old and valuable, and Maelgwn will be furious when I tell him I've lost it.'

Nest was in need of help. She decided to turn to an old friend called Asaph, who knew Maelgwn well. Asaph was now an important bishop.

'Perhaps Asaph can help me,' said Nest. 'I'll send him a letter to tell him what's happened and he can advise me what to do.'

She gave the letter to a messenger who rode off on the fastest horse in the prince's stables. He delivered the letter to the bishop and the bishop replied by return.

Bishop's Palace
Lunchtime

Dear Nest,

Thank you for your letter. I was very pleased to hear from you and to know that you haven't forgotten your old friends, even though you are now a princess.

Don't worry about the ring. Bring Maelgwn over for supper tomorrow night and all will be well. Will seven o'clock be convenient?

Bye for now,
Asaph

P.S. Sorry about the egg stain on this letter. I'm eating my lunch.

That night and all next morning Nest was sick with

worry. Each time she saw Maelgwn, she slid her hand into her pocket in case he or one of his servants noticed that the valuable ring was missing.

At lunchtime she hid her hand under the table and said sweetly, 'I had a letter from Asaph today.'

'Did you? What did he have to say?' asked Maelgwn.

'Not much, but he's invited us over tonight for supper and a chat,' replied Nest.

'Oh, excellent!' said the prince. 'I've got to go and kill a dragon near Conwy this afternoon, so I shall be as hungry as a hunter by supper time.'

Nest was very glad that Maelgwn would be out of the way all afternoon. That evening she made sure she wore gloves for the journey to the bishop's palace. She hoped with all her heart that Asaph would keep his promise, though how he could help her, she couldn't imagine. Maelgwn had a fiery temper and he would be beside himself when he found out that she had been so careless.

Asaph came to greet them at the door of the palace.

'Come inside and sit yourselves down,' he said, leading them towards a great oak table that was laid for supper.

'Thank you, Asaph,' said Maelgwn. 'I'm so hungry after all that hunting, I could eat a horse.'

'Well, I'm afraid that isn't on the menu,' replied the bishop with a mischievous smile. 'All I have is a salmon that was caught at the mouth of the river.'

'That'll do fine,' said Maelgwn. 'There's nothing better this time of year than a salmon fresh from the sea.'

'No, but before we start I have something to tell you,' said Asaph.

Nest's heart sank, as Asaph began telling Maelgwn

the story of the ring. She watched in dismay as her husband's face darkened. In the end Maelgwn could stand it no longer.

'What? You've lost the most valuable ring in the whole of Gwynedd!' he burst out. 'That's it, Nest! That's the last time you go swimming. You're not to go near the sea again!'

'But you haven't heard the end of the story,' said Asaph winking at Nest. 'Anyway we'd better eat first before the supper gets cold.' He rang the bell at his elbow and at once a servant brought in the salmon.

Despite his bad temper Maelgwn had to admire the fish.

'This is a very fine fish indeed,' he said. 'I'm sure it'll be delicious.'

'I'm sure it will,' said Asaph, 'for it was caught close to the very place where Nest went swimming.'

'Huh!' said Maelgwn sulkily.

'Come now,' said Asaph. 'Would you like to cut us a slice each, Maelgwn?'

The prince picked up a sharp knife and cut a portion of salmon for his wife. As he did so, what do you think rolled out of the salmon with a clink and a flash of gold? Yes, the missing ring!

Believe me, Nest enjoyed her supper that night more than anyone.

*　　*　　*

Maelgwn had proved to be a clever young man while still at school. This was of great advantage to him when his father, Cadwallon, died.

'Although you are the son of Cadwallon – may he rest in peace,' said Einion, one of the wise men of Gwynedd, 'that does not mean you will be our next prince. A prince must be very clever and we must choose carefully, so we have invited all young men of royal blood to undergo a test.'

'What sort of test?' asked Maelgwn.

'Come to Aberdovey in a week's time and you shall see,' said Einion. 'There you must prove that you are indeed worthy to be Prince of Gwynedd.'

And so the following week Maelgwn and half a dozen others presented themselves on the beach at Aberdovey.

'As you see, the tide is out,' said Einion. 'But in an hour it will be on the turn and this beach will soon be under water. The next Prince of Gwynedd will be he who stands his ground longest against the waves. Best of luck to you all!'

Some of the competitors began to build huge platforms of sand. Others dug moats to keep the sea away. But what did Maelgwn do? He vanished into the sand dunes and, when he returned at last, he had with him a chair made from plaited marsh grass.

'Are you going to sit down and watch the tide come in?' teased one of his rivals, who was shovelling sand for all he was worth.

'Maybe,' said Maelgwn.

By this time the tide was on the turn and the sea rushing in. It soon flooded the moats and the moat-diggers were the first to flee for their lives. The men on the sand-heaps laughed at them, but not for long. The sea swept over them and one by one the sand-heaps were all washed away. Now there was only one contestant left and that was Maelgwn. He had been clever enough to build a chair that would float on the sea. There he sat comfortably, watching his wet, bedraggled rivals flee for the shore. Gwynedd had found itself another clever prince to follow Cadwallon!

*   *   *

In his court at Deganwy Maelgwn had many maids and servants. Amongst them were eighty poets and harpists whose duty it was to entertain him. The chief harpist was Cadfan and the chief poet was Rheinallt. These two did not get on at all. Maelgwn had noticed this, so one day he took Rheinallt to one side.

'Tell me, Rheinallt,' he said, 'why don't you like Cadfan?'

'Because he taunts me every single day,' replied Rheinallt. 'He says harpists are better than poets, which is nonsense. Then he's forever combing his hair and simpering in front of the mirror. He's a dandy, that's what he is!'

Smiling to himself Maelgwn went back to his room. He wanted to teach Cadfan a lesson and as he was a wise prince, he soon came up with an idea.

'In six months' time we shall hold a competition,' he announced to his court. 'All the poets and harpists of Wales must compete to see who is best.'

Maelgwn saw how spitefully Cadfan looked across at Rheinallt. Once again he couldn't help smiling, but he said nothing.

Soon posters appeared all over Wales:

BY ROYAL COMMAND

A COMPETITION
will take place
between
POETS and HARPISTS
on the first day of November.

GENEROUS PRIZES

Judge: His Royal Highness, Prince Maelgwn

A WARM WELCOME TO ALL
THE MORE THE MERRIER
*Competitors to meet on the riverbank at Deganwy
at 10 o'clock in the morning.*

The river Conwy flowed past Maelgwn's Court in Deganwy. On the opposite bank stood the town of Conwy. It so happened that November the first was a bitterly cold day and the waters of the river were dark with rain. That didn't stop a huge crowd of competitors gathering on the banks. They formed two distinct groups. The poets were noisy and talkative, while the harpists wore colourful clothes and carried their harps on their backs. Rheinallt was in the one group and Cadfan, who was doing his best to keep his court shoes clean, was in the other.

'I can see a boat coming from the direction of Conwy!' shouted a harpist.

'Thank goodness for that,' said Cadfan with a shiver. 'The cold is playing havoc with my fingers.'

As the boat drew close they recognised the oarsman. It was Maelgwn himself.

'I'm very glad to see so many of you gathered here this morning,' he announced as he stepped ashore. 'The competition will take place in a quarter of an hour on top of Conwy Mountain. Good luck, everyone!'

'But how are we supposed to get there?' screeched Cadfan. 'There are no boats to take us.'

'Exactly!' said Maelgwn, jumping back into his own boat. 'I'll see you in a quarter of an hour.'

All the competitors scratched their heads. The only way across was to swim. But how could they do that in November when there was snow on the mountains and the river in flood?

Rheinallt was the first to make a move. He plunged into the icy water and swam towards Conwy. Soon everyone else had followed suit, including Cadfan and his fellow-harpists. Despite the strong current, everyone made it safely to the far bank, though many looked the worse for wear, especially Cadfan and his friends. Their fancy clothes weren't meant for swimming, though their harps had kept them afloat.

After everyone had struggled to the top of Conwy Mountain, the competition began. Soon the poets were in full flow. Despite being soaked to the skin they composed poem after poem. But when the harpists stepped forward, it was a different story. After their dip in the river the harps were silent and many fell to bits. Cadfan himself was in tears after ruining both his harp and his fancy clothes.

In his own cunning way Maelgwn had proved that poets were the best because, no matter what happens, a poet can still write poetry. And from that day on Rheinallt had no trouble with Cadfan!

*   *   *

In those days poets could see into the future and they would write of it in their poems. One day Elffin, one of the court bards, had a vision and this is what he wrote:

'A beast will rise
From Morfa Rhianedd
And avenge all the lies
Of Maelgwn Gwynedd.
Its cruel yellow teeth
And a whiff of its breath
Will lead to the death
Of Maelgwn Gwynedd.'

Maelgwn was terrified when he heard this.

'The strange beast is the Yellow Death,' he said to his wife.

'What on earth is that?' asked Nest.

'It's a dreadful scourge that has come across the seas,' said Maelgwn in a hoarse voice.

'Well, you're an expert at hunting dragons and vipers,' said Nest. 'I'm sure you can kill it.'

'This beast is different. It's worse than your worst nightmare. It has long, sharp, yellow teeth which can tear you apart and it's covered in filthy yellow fur. Even its eyes are yellow.'

'But you can slay it, can't you?'

'No one has managed it yet. They say that the sight of

147

it is enough to kill you. Its breath is deadly too. The beast can even change shape. Sometimes it appears as a shower of poisonous yellow rain that kills all it touches.'

Nest turned pale.

'Where is the beast now?' she asked.

'They say it's coming along the coast and killing everything in its path,' said Maelgwn grimly.

'So it's the end of us, Maelgwn!' cried Nest.

'Not quite, dear wife. If we go to Rhos Church, lock ourselves in and cover every window, we'll be safe. Even the Yellow Death won't dare enter the church.'

So Maelgwn and his family and all his servants locked themselves into Rhos Church, which stood nearby. It was a tight squeeze and not at all pleasant, but anything was better than facing the Yellow Death.

They were there for hours. In the darkness they could see nothing and hear nothing. And then there came a slow rustling noise as if thousands of snakes were dragging themselves over dry land, followed by the sound of a panting and chilling breath.

'It's the Yellow Death!' wailed Nest. 'The Yellow Death is outside!'

Without thinking Maelgwn went to peep through the keyhole. At once he fell flat on his back and, by the time a servant had lit a candle, he was dead. Just as Elffin's poem had foretold, the Yellow Death had killed Maelgwn Gwynedd.

*   *   *

Although it is many hundreds of years since Maelgwn died, Rhos Church still stands between Deganwy and

Llandudno. It's a pretty little church, with many ancient objects, including a gravestone that dates from Maelgwn's time. It isn't Maelgwn's own gravestone, though he was buried in the church.

The remains of Maelgwn's court can be seen nearby on Bryn Maelgwn and if you go towards Aberdovey, you will come to Maelgwn beach where he defeated the waves.

So, as I said at the beginning, if you are called Maelgwn, you should be very proud of your name – the name of a prince of Gwynedd.

*   *   *

And that is the last of the stories in this book, but there are many, many more throughout Wales – dozens, if not hundreds, of tales which you have yet to hear. Why not ask your parents or your grandparents to tell you the stories of your area?

Take a journey through Wales and discover a wealth of folk tales that have entertained generations of children of all ages. The twelve tales in this collection were chosen by John Owen Huws and are retold, for today's children, in his own lively, dramatic style.